WAR
INSIDE ME

WAR
INSIDE ME

Sydney Nicholas

authorHOUSE®

AuthorHouse™
1663 Liberty Drive
Bloomington, IN 47403
www.authorhouse.com
Phone: 1-800-839-8640

First published by AuthorHouse   01/30/2012

ISBN: 978-1-4685-4603-3 (sc)
ISBN: 978-1-4685-4604-0 (hc)
ISBN: 978-1-4685-4605-7 (ebk)

Library of Congress Control Number: 2012901602

Printed in the United States of America

Any people depicted in stock imagery provided by Thinkstock are models, and such images are being used for illustrative purposes only.
Certain stock imagery © Thinkstock.

This book is printed on acid-free paper.

CONTENTS

Acknowledgments

I would like to thank first and foremost my parents for telling me during those hard math nights that "don't worry, you will get it one day, and remember, you will grow up and be a writer". I live by that, I always try but at the end of the day that is what I remind myself. You have loved and supported me no matter what and that means more to me than you will ever know.

To my teachers who never gave up on me. You encouraged my creative mind and writing. Mrs. Toney, who was the first person to ever acknowledge my writing and pointed out in third grade that I needed to be an author, well here I am, you were right.

My friends who understand when I have my hands glue to a book or my laptop and can't hang out with them.

My friends at Stay-Focused, you guys have no idea how much you made me feel good about who I am.

Rue, I know we met by the click of a mouse but when I met you it did not feel like I was meeting a stranger, I was meeting a friend. You have helped me from start to finish, pushed me when I needed it and most of all you love this book as much as I do.

All of you have played a part in shaping who I am today, so thank you and enjoy.

To everyone that has ever had a war inside them.

"For everyone in life there is one person that was made to make it all go away."
-Sydney Nicholas

Preface

Some say everything happens for a reason and after she killed herself I didn't believe them, I said I still don't get the good in my life and it was going down the crapper. I lost hope in words like, God, fate and serendipity. I was blind and lifeless, hell . . . . I was mad at the world. Now I do believe in all words, for nothing is a lie, now that I beat the war inside me.

CHAPTER ONE

Romantic Killer?
Never heard of one

She was my sweetheart and I loved her. Val Vandecamp and I were everything you can ask for. I didn't know where she was but I did hear people talking. Some say she didn't even let her dad turn any lights on in the house if he did, well she would cry. Others say she skipped town and her dad had to drag her back. I even hear people saying she did drugs. I will never know what happened in the two weeks before. Val never let anyone see that she was upset. As for what happened, she killed herself. It wasn't that hard to put together, me of all people knew her the best, better than her own dad. I started with what her dad told me was in the bathroom, a glass and an empty pill bottle. Umm, not that hard to see how she did it, but why? Then my mind drifted and the memory of that call consumed me . . .

"Jude, its Mr. V. I know what time it is, but I had to call. I know she would want me to tell you first." He said with no feeling in his voice.

"Tell me, Mr. V. what is it?" I asked loudly because I was scared out of my mind by now. "Val . . . . she . . . . she . . . . killed herself last night. I'm so sorry."

I couldn't think, I couldn't speak, it was like that guy on the movie "Click" I hit the mute button.

"No, what kind of cruel, sick joke is this?" I asked him with rage in my heart.

"Jude, I am so, so, so sorry, but it's true." He told me and I hit 'end'

*　　*　　*

I tried to think like her, it wasn't like her dad was never around but her mom died in childbirth. She was a very good student, top of our class; she was a shoe-in for USC. It had to be my fault. I would hate myself forever if she killed herself because of me. Yes, I Jude Franklin killed the love of my life. I had to go to our place; I had to feel close to her again. A place that would help me remember . . . perhaps a place to forget . . . because I really want to, forget everything that is. I looked to my Mom and she looked as hollow as I feel.

"Mom, I am going to Sunset Beach." I called back to her, on my way out.

Everyone in my family knows what Sunset Beach means to me, they know the short story anyway, I met Val there . . . . but I also had the best night of my life there . . . a night I would never forget . . . with her. I walked to the spot where I first saw her and closed my eyes, letting my memory take me . . .

Three years ago I recall that I walked out the door that day with a skip in my step. I felt the hot sand on my feet but I didn't care . . . nothing could have made this day bad, yet I still didn't know why I was so happy. I walked out to the water and put my toes in, it was warm, just like the sand. I looked around for a girl that would show me a good time. But all of them were with good-looking guys. I was thinking that everyone had someone but me, and then I saw her.

She was reading a book. I tried to think of things to say to her, anything. I tossed my cup on the ground and went to pick it up at her feet.

"Oh miss, I'm sorry I must have dropped this. Let me do my good deed for the day." I smiled as I picked up the cup.

She then looked up from her book, smiled, and said, "You from around here? I have never seen you before, I would know if I saw a guy with a face like that."

"No, I just moved here from Texas," I told the girl with the bright green eyes.

"Well, looks like you need someone to show you around, now I myself am into this book so I don't think I have the time." she spoke with fire in her eyes at each word.

"Oh that is a shame; I guess I will have to do this." I said taking a step closer to her book that covered her face. I grabbed the book and ran as fast as I have ever run in my life.

I started reading a random page, "Young love is something we never forget it changes us forever. In life we are not sure about a lot of things, but one we are sure of, we know when we fall in love for the first time." I read as I ran when the pretty girl caught up to me she turned red.

"That's mine, just because you're from out of town doesn't mean you can just steal people's things." she said as she took her book from my hand.

"Well, looks like you have to show me how to behave." I winked at her I didn't even know her name at that time and I knew I wanted to spend as much time as I could with her.

"Yes but I don't know how to make a boy behave without saying his name in a mean mom voice and since I don't know your name . . ." she smiled and started to laugh.

"My name is Jude Franklin and you are? Oh I know, the prettiest girl in the world."

"You have a lot of nerve Jude Franklin, just meeting me and hitting on me, all in less than an hour. My name is Val Vandecamp." she said putting out her right hand.

"It's very nice to meet you Val." I said taking her hand in mine and kissing it.

"Maybe I can show you around California, see I was thinking you were a jerk." she said being honest. "Oh I am hurt, but you know what, I will take it. What time?" I asked Val, completely shocked that my cheesy line had worked on her.

*   *   *

Someone tapped me on the back, jerking me out of my daydream and when I didn't turn around she spoke up, "Hey, you look like you're lonely my name is Wendy what is yours?" She asked and I wanted to hit her in the face, dumb girls think they can just walk up and make you fall in love with them, then they get all crazy and mess up your life.

"That's sort of the point now can you go away?" I asked turning around to look her square in the face to show her I am not joking. I looked at her for the first time and if I wasn't hateful and heartbroken, I would so do her, which means it's time to run.

"You know what? I changed my mind, I'll go, and you stay." I yelled as I walked away.

"No, I get it . . . . don't go." She yelled, but it was too late I was already gone. So . . . . so far gone.

CHAPTER TWO

Beast Inside me.

I was in the car and I heard my phone ring and I picked it up.

"Hello Mr. Franklin? This is Jack Rush from the OCSD; we need you to come in for questioning." It hit me like a truck, she killed herself because of me and now as if that wasn't hard enough, they think I killed her with my own hands.

"Okay, I'm on my way." I said. What else could I say, 'no, go to hell?' That would put me in jail for sure.

When I got to the room it was just like on the show CSI, it had the gray table and big windows. I sat down in the chair close to the door just like where the bad guys sit on the show. I heard the door open and Mr. Jackass Rush walked in slowly and sat down across from me, to give me a heart attack no less.

Jack Rush . . . okay, now if you are going to visualize a crappy cop drama this guy has it on lockdown . . . from his thinning hair, to his pot belly and strong stench of cigarette smoke. It kind of irritated me that someone so unappealing would be sitting me down and grilling me . . . I understand it is his job, but it was my life . . . and a girl like Val would never have given this guy the time of day.

"Mr. Franklin, you were Val Vandecamp's boyfriend. Did you have sexual intercourse with Ms. Vandecamp?" He asked and that got me mad because what does that have to do with her case? Did I rape her, no . . . not in a million, billion years. So ask me about her death, fair but ask me about our sex life like it had to do with her death, not okay, not okay at all.

"Yes we did, why, do you want to know how many times?" I asked with force.

"Well . . . just protocol." he said, not helping me feel any less irritated about where this seemed to be going.

"Protocol? . . . listen I have watched a lot of T.V. And that never seems to be a question asked."

"You seem a little aggravated Mr. Franklin."

"It's Jude." I said as the weight of "Mr. Franklin" seemed to much for me.

"Sexual contact is a concern in this case."

"Like a rape?" I asked.

"No . . . no, I apologize for giving that impression."

I looked at him and squinted my eyes.

"Well how else was I supposed to take it?"

"I guess we should just get to the point Jude." he said, adjusting himself on his chair.

"Yes . . . that would be appreciated." I said as I leaned back and crossed my arms on my chest.

"Jude . . . Ms. Vandecamp was due to have a baby when she died. It could have something to do with her death."

"What?" I said as I looked up and stared at him.

"A baby . . . she was pregnant."

The world tilted, I swear that it did . . . like some old movie about a psychotic losing their mind. I felt the sweat start to form on my forehead and that asshole just sat there, with no emotion, tapping his dirty fingernails on the table.

"Mr. Franklin . . ."

I stood up and almost knocked the chair over, clutching at the table to steady myself.

"Mr . . . ."

I looked at him with more hatred than I ever think I have sent out to anyone ever.

"It is JUDE!" I yelled at him.

"I do not think the technicality of your name is the issue." he said all smug and condescending.

"Shut up." I said half out of breath.

"I am sorry . . . but the baby, I would assume you did not know, who else was she sleeping with?"

"What the hell?" I said as I looked at him with disbelief.

"I just need a name, or names Jude." he said.

"Names? . . . go to hell." I said as I started to sway on my feet.

"Val may have been cheating."

I stared him down and fell into the chair. The thought of her cheating ate away at my heart almost as much as her dying did.

"Okay . . . well, I can see you are in no state of mind to talk right now."

"You think?" I said as I tried to compose myself.

"There are a thousand stories in time about the cold heart of a woman Jude, you will not be the first or last to experience that."

I lost my shit at that point and started to yell at him . . .

"Well the baby had to be mine, she would've told me about our baby, Val wasn't the type of person to cheat. She could never cheat!" I stood up quickly and started to walk out. "Mr. Franklin WE ARE NOT DONE HERE!!!" He yelled so loudly at me the whole place could hear I'm sure. "Mr. Franklin I could detain you, if you don't come back." Detective Rush then stood up and started running after me. I stopped in my tracks giving in and going back to the room. "Now son we aren't saying it wasn't your kid but if it wasn't then it could be a factor to Ms. Vandecamp's death. We will get the CSI working on it." Detective Rush said smoothly so I wouldn't snap.

"Can I go now?" I asked as I looked down at my hands, they felt sweaty and I could feel a tremor starting in them.

"Yes, Mr. Franklin you may go for now, but the questions are far from over."

"It's Jude you ass." I said as I walked away.

I walked down the hallway to whispers, at least I could only hope they were whispering and the psychosis was not settling into my brain. I finally made it to my car and banged my hands on the dashboard over and over again until the numbness set in, a welcomed relief to everything.

"Damn it why is my life so messed up?" I yelled to myself, I felt crazy. I turned up my radio the highest to it could go. I sang along to a song I barely knew, it was a sad song and I cried. I felt like a chick on some dumb movie. I wanted to stay right here in my car forever and never come out, but that didn't happen to my dismay I pulled up to my drive way and went into my house, tears in my eyes and all.

"Oh honey what's wrong?" My mom said as she rushed to my side. My family knows I never cry, before now that is. I pushed her away and shut my door loudly.

"I don't want to talk to this family or anyone for that matter, I'll go to work, go to school, do my homework, walk on the beach (with Val, I added in my head) and go to bed. All the rest is meaningless bull shit and can go to hell!!" I yelled as I sobbed but I knew Mom and Joey, that is my little goody-goody brother, could hear every word and that fed the beast inside me. I decided that being home was the last thing I wanted, talking to anyone was the last thing I wanted . . . and leaving was a number one must do. I stood up, ran to my door and swung it open, hoping that my emotional exit would just make them both let me go as I needed to.

I ran past Mom as she reached towards me . . . I cannot allow anyone to try to console me, there is nothing that could be said or done anyway. Time for the destructive side of me . . . in fact it has to happen, especially now. My mind is reeling, visions of Val's face, her lips . . . keep running through my mind, making my heart ache as if the blood cannot reach it.

I needed a beer so I grabbed my wallet, which had my fake ID in it and walked out of the house. I ran to the bar I normally go to named Brix Wines, they never card me but I thought I should take my ID just in case. Although I have to guess, that due to slow business, they must turn a blind eye to minors like me. I grabbed my normal stool at the bar. I knew Drake works on Tuesdays and we are sort of tight. He is the only one that called me out the first time he saw me, he said something like,

"Hey kid, I wasn't born yesterday I made 50 fake IDs in my day, however I like you so you're cool." Ever since then and by then I mean freshmen year, we've been friends. Drake walked up just like I said he would and I would have smiled but smiling is not an option right now.

"Hey man, come to ditch the pain and get back in the game?" Drake asked, I didn't want to be like a baby and say what game, there is no game without her, like I was thinking, no I came up with guy talk, if only I could still walk the walk.

"You know it, brother, I was born ready." I said and held out my hand for that lame hand shake that guys do to look cool.

"Bud Light, am I right?" Drake asked as if he didn't know. I nodded and Drake handed me my beer with a wink.

"So, how are things . . . ?" Drake asked with a worried look. I knew what he meant by 'things' and since Drake is the only person I trust I didn't down play it.

"Life is a truck rolling over me, every time I open my mouth." I told him putting my face in my hands.

"Jude, when I first met you, you were a strong, bright young man that was full of life, I hate to see you like this." He said as he stared at me, You see Val was the first one to show me this place, Drake knew how in love we were, but Drake wants me to move on. I didn't say anything more. I mean, what else is there to say? I finished my beer and asked Drake for number two, he handed it to me without a word.

"Hottie five o'clock, come on man try out some new legs, you'll have fun." Drake pleaded. I finished my beer shortly after he said that and without needing a bill I put money and a good tip on the bar and walked away.

Chapter Three

Being in my happy place is happy, because I am alone.

I went to the beach like always, standing in our spot. It is our spot because this is where we first made love. I closed my eyes and went back to one of the best nights of my life.

"Are you sure we should be out here this late at night? My Dad will kill me if get in trouble with the law, Cowboy." Val said in a small voice letting go of my hand.

She looked up at the moon, "How could something that simple be so pretty?" Val asked me. I stepped forward to catch her in my arms.

"That's what I asked myself when I met you." I spoke in her ear kissing behind it in between words. "How did I get so lucky?" Val smiled that smile that makes your heart stop.

"I can think of more ways to get lucky." I said laughing as I slipped my jacket off. Then I went behind Val to take her jacket off as well.

"Jude we can't, what about protection? What would my dad think?" Val asked all at once. I put my finger to her lips, "Shh honey, let me ask you something, do you love me? Do I make you happy?" I asked looking deep into her eyes and putting my hand on her cheek.

"Yes, yes but I'm scared it's my first time and what if I do something wrong?" Val asked with worry in her eyes.

"Don't think just do, we are learning together." I said holding a condom up to her eyes. I laid down in the sand and pulled her with me. I then rolled over so I was on top of her.

"I want this to be everything you ever dreamed of, when you close your eyes I want it to be me you see. I won't want to have this bond with anyone else." I said before I took her away. I took her dress off and as I dreamed she was breathtaking. I trembled as I unhooked her bra. I ripped open the condom and put it on. I couldn't believe I was making love to such an amazing girl.

"Wow Val, honey slow down, I need a timeout okay, but don't worry you will be in my arms forever." I laughed and kissed her forehead.

"To think I was worried it all seems silly now. I just want to be with you forever." Val said and I will never forget how she looked at me like I was her world. It was the look of love.

"I want to be with you too, I will go anywhere you go. Tonight is what we should focus on right now. I can stay with you tonight. I made something up with my mom. I also got you covered as well. Nicole called your Dad, he thinks you're spending the night there." I told Val with joy knowing for once she was all mine. "Oh Jude how romantic, where will we sleep?" Val asked and as she asked I couldn't help but smile. It took me seven weeks to get the money for the hotel but I did it for her. It was the best night of my life. "We are staying at a hotel here on the beach, the Ramada." I told her with pride.

"Oh sweetie I don't know what to say, that's amazing." Val's eyes lit up and she kissed me. I hated to cut her off so I could call the hotel.

"Yes it's under the name Franklin, No,I will pay in cash, thank you. We should be there at 10:30." I told the man on the phone.

"We have to start walking, I need to leave my car here so my mom wouldn't know, I'm sorry." I told Val as I took her hand.

"Nothing can ruin this night I would walk a hundred miles if you were by my side." Val told me and my heart skipped a beat, like it often did when I was with her.

When we got to the hotel they were shocked we were seventeen,but they took my money after I showed them my I.D. I carried Val up to our room and I didn't care who stopped and looked at my ring finger, looking back I wish we did have rings, something to show our commitment and love for one another. I unlocked the door and opened it with my foot.

"How manly of you baby, oh candles and roses when did you do this?" Val asked surprised. "I came here before I brought you to the beach, told Mom we needed milk." I said with a smile and Val hit my arm that still held her. "You should have told me. Sex, hotel room that you had to spend weeks to afford, roses and candles. I would have packed sexy outfits and not look like this, that's for sure." Val half laughed . . . half cried.

"You look amazing in whatever you wear, I love you for you. Not for what you wear." I told her kissing every part of her body I could find.

*　　*　　*

I walked up to the beach bar and I saw her, that girl, what was her name . . . oh yeah, Wendy. I didn't want any part of her, even for a one night stand, I can't have that.

23

"Hey you, I'm not done talking to you, so can you listen?" She asked and I gave in why not I'll walk away without a word it'll all be okay.

"What . . . I'm listening,why don't you have a sit?" I asked her and that was the closest I would get to being nice, I was sure.

"Sure thanks, I want to tell you a story but I have to tell you it's sad." She looked shocked that I was talking to her, I was too. I shook my head at her.

"Before I came here, I was raped by a guy named Mike, I have never told anyone before and I felt like you needed to hear it. I too have a broken heart." She poured her heart out to me and it scared me.

"I really don't need to know that." I said as I looked everywhere but her.

"I wanted to tell you, you make me feel like I can talk."

"You shouldn't." I said as I started to get up and she grabbed my arm and I looked at her pretty face.

"You are kind, I just know it . . . please." she said and it did tug at my heart for a moment and instead of closing myself off completely I looked at her and smiled.

"Thank you, the name's Jude." I told her and walked away.

"Wait, Jude I'm not giving up, I got time!!!" Wendy called after me, and I wanted to go to her . . . but I couldn't.

"Don't." I said as I walked away.

CHAPTER FOUR

Earthquake on Planet Jude

I don't know why but I can't stop thinking about her, she doesn't know me at all yet she saw me in pain and opened up. Now I am not dumb I know how minds work, if she opens up to me that makes me want to open up to her. In normal Earth, but I don't live there, yes you may think I'm crazy, I live on planet Jude and in my world it doesn't work like in some Nicholas Sparks' movie. I fell for a pretty and smart California girl, but what wasn't on her Facebook was that she was going to take a baby and break my heart by killing herself. So I've learned to not judge a book by its cover, or have the easy way out and not look at the cover to even judge it.

I believe in God, he has a plan but I don't know if I like his plan. I mean when it is up to fate and when is it up to me? I tried to think back to one of the long hours that Val dragged me to church.

*   *   *

"Today I would like to talk about love and God because both are such a big part of life. The Bible once said, 'Whoever does not love does not know God, because God is love.' If you, like many of us have been mad or feel alone, go to God he will give you the tools and make you feel better after you have told him." I recall the minister saying something along those lines. "Which brings me back to the core of our topic to back up my lesson, the Bible states that, Cast your cares on the lord and he will sustain you; he will never let the righteous fall." I was so glad he stopped talking,I hated this but it made Val happy, so what do I have to lose? I looked at her and she looked so peaceful and so damn pretty . . . the rest of the ministers words started to fade away and all I could see was her, I should have listened that day . . . I should have, but I didn't . . .

*   *   *

Well I'll be damned if church didn't just teach me something, maybe one day I won't just go to make a girl happy, maybe one day I will want to go for me. Then again how can I believe in something when my life is so screwed up? That is like telling a dog to drink milk and telling a cat to swim, it just can't happen.

I was too drunk to go home, so I slept right in the sand and with what cash I had in my pocket, I got a sheet from a store to sleep with.

I had to be dreaming that much I knew, as she looked down at my body and stroked my face, "Wake up sleepy head, look around everyone is laughing. How could you sleep on the beach, I mean I know you miss me but live your life baby." Val told me undressing me with her eyes, as she kissed me. Damn I have to be dreaming why did my mind have to hold a knife to my heart?

"Cowboy, do you want to make this a nude beach? Sounds like this had happened before, but I've never had an audience, it's kind of sexy." We were in the water next thing I knew and I wasn't sure I was dreaming anymore. Maybe I'm in heaven. But how did I die?

"Who gives a damn, you're with me." she whispered.

"Really, really, Valerie baby, IT IS YOU!!" I yelled

Water hit my face and the light came on, I felt dizzy.

"Oh Jude, I have you its okay." I knew the voice but it wasn't hers, Wendy was in my dream? Oh I must be crazy, why can't I wake up? This must be hell. Someone slapped me on the face hard, I blinked and I saw Wendy holding me, I was wet and crying.

"Why the hell are you here?" I asked

"You were walking into the water shouting things, and a girl's name, umm, Valerie." She told me stroking my face.

"You could have been killed, I think you were sleepwalking." She added, sounding scared for me. I nodded.

"I think I am losing my mind." I whispered almost to low for her to hear.

"What?" she asked me as she took my arm and gently held it.

"I saw her . . . I did . . ." I said more to myself than to her.

"Jude." Wendy said and I looked at her through blurred vision.

"You look terrible . . . you really do."

"I feel worse than I look." I said.

"Come on I'll buy you shirt at my mom's shop." She said putting me on my feet. I started to walk and I felt dizzy again Wendy put her arm around me so I wouldn't fall. Normally, I would shake her off but I was scared and cold I needed someone, no I needed Wendy she understands me. I have to let her in, I have to know this amazing woman, this is scary but I have to do it.

CHAPTER FIVE

Change of heart, well maybe

Wendy led me to her mom's shop, and I felt like I shouldn't meet her mom. What if she thinks we are a thing? I can't run out on the girl who just saved my life and I know I want to get to know her but this is a lot to handle, way too soon. Still shirtless and cold, I wanted to run back to the beach and cry. I could put a hat on and block the sun to sleep. I don't know why but something inside me just couldn't run. I looked at Wendy and I saw that she was hot,even in dumb running shorts and a sports bra. She was kind to the core and something made me want to be the man I used to be, so I could be with her. Wendy started to grab this shirt, that shirt, and finally settled on one for me. I liked the shirt she picked out for me, it was made like a rashguard.

"Mom, this is Jude, I found him, umm, on the beach . . . he was cold." Wendy said it and I knew her mom was judging me, this is why me and people don't mix, oh come on Jude, try even if you have to kiss the ladies' ass, show her you're not some beach bum.

"Yeah, Wendy saved my life, I fell asleep on the beach last night and I was sleepwalking in the water. You raised her right, Wendy's mom." I sounded good right up till the ending when I didn't know Wendy's last name. "Ms. Brandsworth, but you can call me Carrie." Carrie smiled at me and I felt good about her, now for Wendy let's just hope I can open up, it won't be easy but I can't be alone.

"Sure thing, Carrie and thanks for the rashguard, I'll have to keep this store in mind, I do some surfing and diving myself." I said and bingo she lit up, and smiled taking the bate.

"So does Wendy, she has never been in the California sea, and I surf but don't dive, maybe you could repay her that way." She eyed me and Wendy blushed.

"I did what any person would do, I don't need to be repaid . . . saving Jude was an amazing feeling." She said giving her mom a mean look, if this works and I can open up, I'll take her diving because I can tell she wants to.

"Well I'm needing a Coke and fries, will you join me?" I asked Wendy in hopes that I didn't mess up before I even got started. I looked at her with sparkling eyes. She smiled and as it often did when I was with Val, my heart stopped and I smiled a bright big smile, it felt amazing, to know I was ready to open up, and possibly allow love back in.

That was a scary thing, I am scared of trusting everyone and I am going to trust a woman with my heart? Well let's just slow down, I just met her, but I can't help it, I have this need to love someone with all my heart. We walked out of the shop and Wendy took her arm off of me, as I could hold my own weight now that I am no longer in shock.

"Is the bar okay? I have a fake ID and you look like you could pass, not saying you have to drink, I meant it when I said Coke." I smiled it wasn't the best pick up line the world has ever seen but I had time.

"Okay that sounds good sure." Wendy agreed and we sat down.

"Two Cokes, and a plate of fries, thanks." I told the bartender.

"So Jude, tell me who is this Val?" She asked and I was taken back, I'm sure she could see it on my face and she waited, she didn't back down, I like that.

"Valerie Lee Vandecamp was the love of my life, two weeks ago she killed herself and it's been hard. I have been pushing everyone away. When I met you I was in a dream like state and I was mad you woke me up and she was gone." I told her, being scared I might tear up. Wendy put a hand on mine and I knew this was it, and this is crazy believe me, I know, but I had the drive to love her for the rest of my life.

"Jude I am so sorry, I had no idea, I mean I push people away too and it's the hardest thing I have ever done, but you, that's not something I could live with." Wendy said from the bottom of her heart.

"Tell me about him, about what happened." I pushed her a little bit, I opened up to her so she can open up to me right? Maybe it's a little too soon, we all have a way of getting over things right? This is big step for her and I don't know her, yet.

"Umm, I was getting gas at 11 p.m, when some kid from my school came up, drunk, and started talking to me, I told him it had been a long day and to get lost. I turned my back and he put a hand to my mouth, a friend of his came up from behind him and put a gun to my head. I didn't cry, I didn't try to yell, I just looked around and there was no one else in sight. I never even saw his face. He took a part of me I can never get back. For weeks before I came here I tried to tell myself I liked it, that girls like me don't get raped. I gave up he was a monster and if I was strong I would kick his ass in court." Wendy half yelled "I could come with you, I know how scary things can be when people don't understand, I want to be the person you come to, because I need someone that understands too." I said smiling at how easy it was to talk to her, and I don't do this deep shit, or I should say I didn't except with Val.

"I have never met a guy like you, Jude." Wendy said and my heart thudded. I stepped closer to her and wrapped my arms around her and

35

my lips inches from hers, I closed my eyes, and suddenly I could hear Val's voice echoing in my mind . . ." Jude don't do it, Jude I will come for you, wait for me . . . . wait . . . . for . . . . me."

I pulled away from Wendy.

"I'm sorry . . . . I . . . . um . . . . have to go, I'll umm call you." I said as I walked away.

"But, Jude you don't have my . . . ." I didn't even look at her hurt face, I couldn't. I wish I could be everything I want to be for her, but if I can't even kiss her . . . . it can't work.

CHAPTER SIX

To be or not to be,
that is the question

I couldn't help but replay the 'almost kiss' in my head, how it felt to be close to her and that look in her eyes, Val gave me that melted look on Sunset Beach when I told her we could be together for the best night of my life. I know, it's only been like two weeks, since the love of my life killed herself, but it is like Wendy is an EMT and shocked me back to life. So what's the deal? Some of you might say, go after her, are you crazy? Love comes in time of need, I know I need love, but am I letting Val down by doing so? Or would she want me to be happy? My worry is . . . is it love? Or loneliness just beckoning me to Wendy . . . is it the girl or the tragic situation that is driving me now . . .

I walked into the house and upstairs to my room. I closed the door hard so my family knew I was still mad because of what happened the day before and to not push me. I heard the phone ring on my nightstand, I looked at the caller ID, and it was Val's dad. I picked it up, half tempted to not answer it, but my natural instinct pushed the button before I really had a moment to think it through.

"Jude, its Brice I was cleaning out her room and well I found something you need to see for yourself, can you be here in five?" Mr. V. asked. It sounded important and I sure as hell don't want to be at home. "Sure, Mr. V. I'll see you in five." I answered him happily. Finally, I can talk to someone about this mess.

"Oh and Jude, it's Brice now, I consider you family."

"Sure, sure" I hit end and closed my eyes and the ghost of Val consume me yet again . . .

*   *   *

It was a day in bed and Val and I were laughing and talking about life, everyday with Val was my best day and looking into her care-free eyes, I knew it was the right time and place, I would be 18 in May and it was April, Val just turned 18 two weeks before, everyone knew this was coming. I got off the bed, felt the ring in my back pocket and pulled it out, behind my back. I got down on one knee and felt the tears escape my eyes.

"Val, growing up without a dad, Mom always told me to respect women and that one day, I will look into my girlfriend's eyes and realize I can't get up from that spot without knowing that everyday she will get up too, and follow me. Today was that day, I love you Val, and I want to know that wherever I am, you will get up from that same spot in the world with me. Will you marry me?" I asked as I pulled the ring out from behind my back and opened the black box with a smile full of tears. She said nothing, she slid down to the floor, where I was still on one knee and kissed me, knocking the ring on the ground.

I pulled away, "Is that a yes, Ms. Vandecamp?' I asked with a laugh.

"Would I get up from that spot if I didn't know you were going to follow me?" She quoted me with a smile. I grabbed the ring and put it on her finger, where it belonged.

*   *   *

I walked out the door of my house without a word, Joey and Mom won't even care, that I was gone and if they did well, too bad. Val's house is a mile from mine so I wanted to walk and burn off some energy, if it is too dark when Mr. V. and I were finished he could drive me home.

I got to the door right on time and let myself in.

"Hey Jude, I'm in her room, come and we can talk!" Mr. V. yelled so I could hear him, I did as I was told. I was scared to see Val's room, but Mr. V. needed me . . . so I walked in with a smile on my face. Mr. V. didn't say a word, but he handed me a piece paper and I sat on her bed and started to read.

> Dear Jude,
>
> I want to start off by letting you that I love you and everything I had ever said to you was true. By now I'm sure that you know, my Dad knows . . . . hell everyone knows that I was pregnant Jude. I want you know that it was ours Jude, our baby. I should have told you, but something inside of me would not let me do it . . . in fact I went to the clinic, but I was too far along to end it. I am not that girl Jude; I am not the have a baby at 18 girl. My Dad would kill me, and despite the fact that I love you more than anything in the world . . . I am taking the only out I think I can now. I know it seems selfish Jude, in fact I know it is . . . but the shame of this is too much for me to bear. My Dad and everyone he knows will be disgusted with me. In fact Jude, if I was to have this baby, my Dad would take it away from me, away from you . . . he would never allow me keep it and I cannot live with that . . . I just can't.
>
> Jude, it's okay to live and be happy, to fall in love again, get married and have kids of your own. You are the best man I ever have known and any girl would be crazy not to marry you. If

I could redo that day you asked me to marry you, I still would have gotten up, but I would have gotten married that day. Jude, don't let life get you down, be the man I fell in love with and never be scared of what I would think.

I have a friend that is amazing, you will meet her soon and I know this will work, it's like she was made for you. I sent her to help you but she needs help too, but ask her why I don't like to gossip. Her name is Wendy; fall in love with her Jude, its better this way.

With all my heart,
Val

PS Don't be mad at Wendy she is just doing what she was told, I even set up her mom with a job and everything, so be mad at me if you have to. I will always be looking out for you.

My stomach turned over and I held my mouth as I swear I thought I was going to hurl all over the floor.

"Oh my God, Brice did you read this?" I asked, still in shock. He nodded

"What are you going to do, Jude?" He asked with a worried look.

"I'm going to call Wendy, we almost kissed hours ago but I ran away because I was scared Val would be hurt if she knew, but she wasn't hurt." I said as I walked to the kitchen and looked in the phone book, I put the phone up to my ear.

"Hello, this is Carrie Brandsworth may I ask who's calling?" She asked in a friendly voice.

"It's Jude Franklin, Val Vandecamp's ex boyfriend and I know Val sent her. I want to talk to her, may I?" I asked in the same tone I use with Mr. V.

"Umm sure." I heard Ms. B. yell for Wendy.

"Hey Jude what's up?" she asked in a good mood. "I was wondering when you would call." Wendy said in an all-too-knowing voice.

"I read a letter from Val today, she told me that you and I are meant to be together." I told her with no life in my voice. "Did you come here knowing we would fall in love as Val said? How do you know Val?" I questioned her.

"You're in love with me?" Wendy asked in a small and shocked voice.

"I'm was falling for you, but what does it matter if we are a lie? I can't believe after all I've been dealing with, I let YOU into my life!" I yelled and felt my heart hurt.

"Not just anyone, no I picked you." I added coldly.

"I was told by Val you needed a friend, I didn't know we were going to hit it off this quick. I want to work with you on this everyday of our lives, this isn't going to be easy for you or me." Wendy said with that voice that makes my heart stop beating.

"I cannot believe this." I said as I closed my eyes and tried to ignore the feeling in my heart.

"Jude, please. I loved Val, I did and she asked me to help you."

"Oh like some fucking charity case huh?"

No . . . oh god, no!" Wendy said as she started to cry.

"I don't need this shit, I really don't and you lied, you lied!" I yelled at her.

"I am so sorry Jude . . . if you hate me, then, say it now."

I paused, knowing I should say goodbye to her, goodbye to all of this, I so know I should. This is crazy, too much for me to digest, I can't . . . and Wendy interrupted my thoughts of telling her to go to hell.

"Jude . . . love is not always what we think it should be, and I am not saying that I love you now . . . but my heart is saying it could be . . . this could be it." she whispered.

I half laughed at her words. "Oh yes, just like Val loved me . . . why am I not shocked that you are her friend?" I said as mean as I could and then I heard it, a quiet crying and damn if it didn't made my heart hurt.

I took a breath and waited for my anger to settle down.

"Wendy." I said all low and exhausted.

"Yes?" she said as she sniffled.

"I have to say Val was my best friend and the love of my life, she worried about me, I want to try too but Wendy, no more lies." I broke down and gave in.

"Agreed we have to trust each other with everything if this is going to work. I just want you to know Jude, Val begged me not to tell you till you found her letter." Wendy added so I would put it to rest.

"Meet me, at Sunset Beach in a hour, I need answers this is a lot to take in, my girlfriend killed herself because of our baby then sent me an angel to fall in love with so she didn't feel bad about crushing my soul, it's all messed up." I sobbed

"What an egocentric bitch!!" I added with gavel in my voice.

"Really Jude she wasn't being self-centered, she was being selfless." Wendy said in a low voice.

"Five in counting Wendy . . . meet me or I will never talk to you again." I said with no life in my voice and I wasn't even sure if she heard me before I hit 'end'.

CHAPTER SEVEN

Doing the Job

I ran to Sunset Beach, still mad, hurt, and needing to run it off. I do this sometimes when things get hard, it clears my head. I got to the bar on the boardwalk; it was nearest to the beach so I was sure Wendy would see me.

"Water?" the waiter guessed, looking at my red face with a smile.

I smiled back; he didn't know what kind of day I was having. It was a good guess for a runner, but not for me, and not today.

"What time is it?" I asked, the poor guy surely would fall for this joke.

"2:30, why?" the guy asked. I just smiled as this was something Dad would do and a waiter should know.

"No, it's beer-thirty." I laughed . . . the guy looked upset by my joke, I pulled my wallet out of my pocket, understanding why this guy looked mad right away.

"Here's my ID" I said coolly.

"Thanks for understanding man, we have to do this to everyone." He laughed, trying not to make it a big deal, some people get pissed when you card them, and I don't because I never get caught.

He checked my ID and handed me a Miller Light.

"Hey Jude." Wendy said, as she smiled

"Wendy, Start . . . From . . . The . . . Top." I said coldly, so she knew I meant it.

"Really Jude, still." Wendy said.

"I need to know the truth." I told her looking deep in her eyes so she knew I meant it. She blushed and I found myself happy that I made her do that.

"I met Val when she came to my town for spring break, her friends wanted to catch some waves and went to my mom's shop. Val didn't want to surf and sort of kept to herself, as I did with you. I went over to her and talked to her. She called me the next day and told me where she was staying and she asked if I would stop by and I said sure. We talked for what seemed like hours, she told me a lot about you and her dad. I told her about my life in Florida with my mom and visiting my dad in London. It didn't seem like she had a bad life, we talked off and on that week, she was in Cocoa Beach then I didn't hear from her after she went home, it wasn't till two years later I heard from her again. The night she killed herself and two weeks before I moved here, but at the time I didn't know her call would change the lives of so many people. She made the call at 2am. She told me about the baby and her fears for it. I tried for an hour to talk her out of her plan and called her every name in the book, but I knew it wouldn't work. I asked her why she called to tell me such heart sinking news. She said because she needed me to swear with my hand on the good book, as this was her dying wish. She told me that I was to watch over you and befriend you so you could cope, she also said she wanted me to be your soul mate, but only if it was right for both of us. Now I know she knew it was right, but she wanted this to be all us and not her plan."

Wendy told me all she knew and I couldn't believe it, all Val said in her letter was true but Wendy said it in a way I could understand. I hope one day you will understand. Little did Val know the day that would be was the day I read her letter.

"Holy shit." I said as I stared at my beer in my hand.

Wendy looked at me nervously.

"I know, it sounds crazy . . . but when she begged me and told me how hurt you would be I found myself drawn to the idea of helping you."

I looked at her coldly. "I don't need anyone to help me. I am not a pathetic case that you feel like you have to save."

"I never ever thought that Jude, I didn't."

"Wendy . . ."

She touched my hand and I looked down at it like it was the worse thing she could do. She removed her hand and rubbed her neck feeling awkward, as she should. I suddenly felt bad for her. I mean, here she is in the same messed up situation as me and just as damaged in some ways as I am. I set my beer down and turned to her.

"I don't hate you."

"You act like it."

"I know, I am just . . . . I don't know what to think here."

Wendy sighed and looked at me, her eyes lingered on my lips for a moment making me feel a bit uncomfortable and I adjusted on my seat. She stopped looking at my lips and looked into my eyes. She did have a pretty face . . . much more so than I had noticed before. Her eyes were a chocolate brown, inviting and pure. It took my breath away for moment. I had to blink to break her charm over me and she spoke.

"If you could only understand how it was to be on the phone with her that night, she was crying and she said the most beautiful things about you and how she loved you."

I laughed, not wanting to hear that at all.

"Sure . . . she loved me alright."

"No . . . Jude, she did, more than anything, I believe that and from what she said . . . you should have known it was true."

"People who love you do not kill themselves and set you up on a date, that is the last thing someone would do."

Wendy looked at me and grinned. "Val was not just "anyone", you know that Jude."

I had to sit back and I found myself playing with the beer in my hand, I then tipped it and it spilled all over the bar and Wendy took her hands from the bar quickly and shook them as beer dripped from her fingertips.

"Oh god . . . I am sorry." I said as I stood up and waved the waiter to us. I took his towel and started to wipe her hands and she watched me as I did. Her skin was warm and inviting and I wanted to say something nice to her for a moment and then stopped myself.

"Jude." she said quietly. I looked at her as I sat back down.

"Please, give me a chance . . . will you go out with me?"

I sat there and weighed the option of what saying 'no' would mean. Then I let my mind wander and a memory came back to me about Val, as they often do now.

*   *   *

I heard the door bell ring and I got up to answer it. It was Val, in jean shorts that would make any guy's mouth water and a V-neck black T-shirt that showed her boobs.

"Hi it's me, Val, from the beach. Well, what you said really stuck to me and well I wanted to give you this." Val said before she kissed me, I could not believe it, it was so unnatural and I loved it.

"Well there you have it, boyfriend." Val said as she kissed me on the cheek and pulled away. "Call me." She added and with that she was gone. It was so simple but it was something I would never forget the way she carried herself, you never knew what she was going to do next.

*   *   *

"Jude? . . . Jude?"

I snapped out of my stupor and stared at her.

"I'm sorry, what?" I said to her.

"Can we . . . . go out?" she asked me in a soft voice.

I looked at her and tried to give her a genuine smile and perhaps it was the mixture of the beer and memory of Val talking but I nodded and said "yes".

CHAPTER EIGHT

A date from girlfriends past

I won't say that I wasn't nervous because I was. It is so stupid to be this worked up over a date with a girl that I just met, but the reasons escaped me. I swear I picked up my phone no less than 10 times, ready to cancel . . . and I should, I know that I should. I mean what the hell am I doing? This girl has my head spinning and I have no idea if I have had a mental breakdown or if I am becoming a freak of sorts. I stood in the mirror and stared at myself and shook my head.

"What am I doing?" I said out loud and then my phone rang and it was Wendy. I looked at it and thought to myself 'What the hell do I say? Thanks but no thanks?' Then I pressed the button and answered it and heard her voice and for some reason it calmed me down instantly.

"Are you just about ready?" she said calmly and I sighed and then swallowed, realizing that a date was going to happen, maybe it needed to.

"Yes, are you?" I asked her.

She laughed. "Jude, you sound nervous, are you?"

"No . . . no, I'm good."

"Okay then . . ."

Then the doorbell rang and I smiled as I hit 'end' on the phone and ran, all excited like a chick on prom night. I stopped and adjusted my shirt before I opened the door up to see her smiling face.

"Hi." she said.

"I would say that was a creeper move, calling me from my porch."

"I had to be sure you were still coming." she said and I felt bad for a moment, like she was some kind of psychic.

"Of course I am going, why would I not?" I said to her.

"Well . . . lots of reasons." she added and she is right. This is a match made in hell, but I like the way it makes me feel to have someone look at me . . . someone who reminds me of the way Val did. Bad way to start a date, I know it . . . but no one said I was sane, least of all me.

We drove in the car and nothing was said. I would have normally been joking and making some kind of conversation, but I can't seem to find that right now . . . the conversation thing that is. We stopped at the top of a hill, overlooking the sea and she shut the car off and I sighed as she opened up her door and stepped out, leaving me no choice but to follow her. I stepped out and looked to my right and saw a blanket, with candles lit and wine and cheese set out and smiled. She had put some effort into this and the least I could do is give her some words, even if they might possibly be empty.

"Wow." I said as I walked up to the blanket and looked down at it. Wendy turned to me and for split second I saw Val's face and it made my heart skip a beat. I took a breath and blinked and Wendy was Wendy again and I tried to not feel guilty, but it was hard to do.

She tapped on the blanket as she sat down and I sat down, trying to smile, but it was kind of fake. I can't help it. She smiled as she pulled out the glasses and started to pour wine into one, handing it to me.

I smiled as I took it and with one big gulp I swallowed it all and she raised her eyebrows and watched me and then smiled as she poured her own glass. I lowered the glass and looked at her and she giggled.

"What?" I asked her.

"You are nervous, it is cute."

"Am not." I said all defiant.

"Okay, if you say so." she said as she sipped her wine and I picked up the bottle and filled my glass, sure that the alcohol would calm me down.

I drank it again and half way through the glass I lowered it, realizing that she was watching me. I half choked and she leaned forward and I leaned back and she relaxed and looked a little hurt that I had moved away from her.

"So." I said.

"So."

I tapped my fingers on the blanket and looked up.

"Nice night."

She laughed and looked up too.

"Yeah, it is."

I looked over at her and the moonlight looked so pretty on her skin that it held my attention for a moment and then I quickly took another drink as she looked at me.

"Jude . . . I am so sorry." she said and with that my heart started to ache again.

"I know." I said, although I didn't know if she actually was or not. I mean, I don't know her, I don't know her at all.

Wendy set her glass down and stared at her hands and I felt compelled to try . . . at least give her something that would make this less awkward.

"I really like the cheese."

Wendy laughed and looked at the cheese and then back to me.

"Okay . . . cheese is good, I guess."

"I mean . . . oh shit, well . . . I like cheese, I could eat it all of time."

"Like a mouse?" she said and I laughed.

"Yeah . . . God, ya know . . . I should go. I just feel stupid."

Wendy reached out and touched my arm and I felt her warm skin against mine and for a moment I felt human again, alive again and less radioactive and alien to the world. I looked at her and she smiled, without parting her lips and I felt like a kiss should happen, but why? If I kiss her the whole thing changes right? I mean she will think we are together . . . and maybe together, or at least the idea is what I need.

"You are so pretty." I said to her, and I did mean it.

"You think so?"

"I do, I really do." I said as I leaned forward and so did she.

I let my lips touch hers and for a moment everything seemed normal, I forgot about Val, I forgot about all the crazy and most of all . . . I forgot about what Wendy had said to me, in fact I didn't care. Then it happened . . . Val creeped into my mind and a memory washed over me as Wendy kissed me with more passion than I could give back to her . . .

*   *   *

She picked me up wearing a black dress that should be on the body of a hooker but at the time of zits and bad teeth, she made me go crazy. We went to a place on a boat to see the sunset and have dinner, that's when I knew she was not only sexy and smart, but down-to-earth as well.

Growing up I always said that everyone thinks like me but I found out later in life people don't think like me, people look in the now not in the later. I want a wife and kids. Why care about grades to the point of madness, when I know what I want to do and where I want to live? My dream is to live in Texas so I can be close to my side of the family, I want my kids to know them. I want to write for the newspaper about loved ones dying and have people write in. I had poured my heart out to Val as she sat there on the boat and played with her hair, looking up at the sky. In fact, I did not know if she heard me at all. Here I am acting like the girl and Val was ignoring me. I cleared my throat and she looked at me all cute as always, making me feel less irritated and more flustered.

"Jude, someday we should have a boat." she said to me.

"I will get you whatever you want." I said back to her.

"We don't need to worry about money."

I swallowed and relaxed in my seat, and I knew it was true, but it kind of made me pissed off just the same.

"I will make money." I said to her.

She smiled and flipped her head, making her long hair fall over her shoulder. She turned slightly and peeked back at me.

"Undo this." she whispered.

I stood up and walked to her, steadying myself as the boat rocked slowly. I reached to her strings on her back and started to pull them and she stood up, making her top fall off and stared at me. I tried to keep my eyes on hers but the temptation to look at her boobs was overwhelming.

Then she dove over the side, under the black water and I started to try to pull my shoes off and I fell as clumsy does . . .

"Jude?"

I opened my eyes and saw Wendy in front of me and for a moment I thought she was the dream and could still smell the salt in the air and the cool breeze on the boat.

"I need to go . . . I'm sorry." I said as I stood up and walked away from her, with no worry of walking home, in fact I needed too. Wendy should just go back to her world, I know this but I have no idea if I am going to let her.

CHAPTER NINE

One beer and a girl should clear things up

I spent the next few days ignoring Wendy's calls and for good reason. I did not want her, in fact the only thing I wanted was to get laid and not by her . . . not by someone who looked so warm and real. I needed random and random was what I would find.

"Hey man."

I pulled out my stool and sat down trying to act like I didn't storm out the last time I was here.

"Hi Frank, Bud Light?"

I nodded at him with a small smile, hoping that isn't over doing it.

"You were right . . . . ."

See it wasn't that hard.

"Huh, I'm sorry, I've slept since then, what was I right about?"

So it wasn't that big of a deal to him, thank God he drinks on the job.

"You told me I should be more like you."

To put it mildly, but I didn't want to piss him off. I needed him to do something for me.

"Yeah, that sounds about right, you are too much like a chick. I mean, really man? Grow a pair."

In an odd way Drake was dead on, I grew up with a mom that told me the way to a woman's heart, not the way to unbutton her pants.

"I need your help, I call upon you, oh mighty Drake."

We laughed together and I knew that I got my best friend back and I would take that over some dumb chick any day, that and the fact that he gives me beer.

"Okay, if you are saying what I think you are, than we need to get you a woman, and I have just the one in mind."

"Who is she?"

"Oh you don't know her but trust me when you see her, you will wish you did."

I trusted Drake. He always had the best leftovers and his Tuesday backed out. Drake showed me photos of her. Man, if I got his Tuesday that would be some gift but I don't think they are on the best terms. When she cut ties, she told him that he was the worst she ever had most of them at least try to act like it's not all about sex.

"Jude, I'd like you to meet Jenna."

Drake put Jenna's hand into mine. I looked her over; she had a light blue cocktail dress on that went perfectly with her light brown skin. She wrapped her curly hair around her finger as she waited for me to speak.

"H-hi Jenna, I hear you are quite the riot."

"Yeah, I try."

This is almost as bad as my date with Wendy. I need to get things moving. Drake, who saw the look on my face, gave me a wink.

"Jenna, I bet Jude would love to see your Porsche."

"Yeah, I have always wanted one but I'd need a lot of cash . . . ."

I got down from my stool and trying to be a gentleman, I helped Jenna down.

I grabbed my jacket from the back of the stool before walking with Jenna out the door.

Jenna had a lime green Porsche; it was the most amazing car I had ever seen.

"Wow."

"That's what I said the first time I saw it too."

"How'd you get it?"

I mean people in Cali have a lot of money but people Jenna's age are still paying college bills.

"Oh daddy loves cars, if you think that's amazing you should see our Lambo."

Ha, I found my way in, I'll take it.

"Can I see it?"

"I thought you'd never ask."

We drove to her family's house which happened to be near Val's. Jenna lead me to the biggest garage ever. There was Ferrari's in just about every color. The Lambo that Jenna talked about had everything in it.

"Can I go inside?"

"Sure."

I walked up to the car. 'Car' is hardly a word I would use, this was not a car, it was a work of art. Jenna pointed to the dashboard.

"You can sync music from your iPod and play it anytime, you don't even have to have it with you, see?"

She plugged in her phone and hit sync, music began to play after she took out the phone.

"It's amazing."

She put her hand on my face.

"It sure is."

She started to kiss me and before I could register that it was happening, it was too late to fight it. I give in, as she pulled out a condom without even breaking the kiss she handed it to me. I had to break the kiss to put it on not even a second after I did, she pushed herself on me with force. I didn't want to stop and that shocked me. We went at it a couple more times then I told her I had to go.

"Awe really?"

"Yes, maybe I'll give you a call but don't hold me to it."

"I know, that's how all Drake's set ups are, you would think by now I would tell my brother to actually find someone that will stick around but the truth is, I really like knowing that if I don't like the guy I don't have to see him again. However it sucks when I really like the guy, like you."

I didn't know what to say, it made me mad that Drake had me do his sister, it's like wrong and gross. Also I hated the fact that every girl even this whore likes me. Jenna asked if I needed a ride and as much as I would love to ride in this car, I can't, no. I would walk and sit on the beach.

CHAPTER TEN

Should have called

I walked in the house trying to be quiet but Mom was making eggs.

"JUDE DAVID FRANKLIN!!!" My mom turned to face me.

"Yes, ma'am?" I asked with my head down like a baby.

"Why didn't you come home last night?" She asked all at once.

I find myself stammering . . . it is something that I do with my Mom and I wish that I didn't.

Then without hesitation I said it. "I stayed with a girl . . . I don't even remember her name but that is none of your business."

"You had a one night stand?" she asked me, crossing her arms across her chest.

"Well, not really, I might see her again."

"Fine, I guess I can't do anything but if you knock her up, I'm not helping." Mom walked back to finish the eggs.

"Well, Mom, I use condoms and I'm not that dumb."

"Yes, you are if you were smart you wouldn't have sex with a random chick."

"Well I'm fucked up so say what you want, Mother, I wish I could bring her back but I can't. NO ONE CAN FIX ME!!"

"Jude." my Mom said and I left her, not caring what else she had to say.

I walked in to Joey's room and sat on his bed.

"Hey, what's up?" I asked him with a smile.

"What's it to you?" My brother asked "You haven't been around for a week." He told me coldly.

"It's been hard man, I'm sorry."

"Like you are the only person in the world with problems."

I sat there for a moment thinking about that . . . and Val . . . . always back to Val.

"Well, whatever, have a good life. I don't care." Joey turned away from me.

"Joey . . . ." I started to say and he looked back at me.

"You have a family . . . . why don't you start acting like that instead of sleeping around with random girls?"

I took a deep breath and let it out slowly . . . calming myself.

"I know I suck . . . I said I was sorry, give me a break." I said.

Joey laughed and walked out not even dignifying me with a response and perhaps he should. I sucked with Val, almost as much as I suck being a brother to Joey.

CHAPTER ELEVEN

The date from hell

I walked into my room and felt my phone ringing in my pocket I slid my finger across the screen and put the phone at my ear before I even thought it through.

"Jude?" Wendy asked me, sounding worried.

"Hi." I said back, wondering why I answered the damn phone at all.

"Is everything okay? I mean you never called me after we . . ." she started to say.

"I am fine, what do you need?" I asked her.

She hesitated and I knew I had been hurtful, I felt it . . . that asshole feeling coming over me.

"Nothing . . . I guess."

"I am sorry."

"You seem to say that a lot Jude."

I grinned and sat down on my bed. "Only to you every single time I talk to you."

"Yes." she said and with that she just let it linger there. I took a breath and decided to attempt to be nice to her.

"So . . . . how have you been?" I asked her, sounding so generic.

"Oh gee, I don't know Jude . . . just awesome I guess." she said, making me laugh under my breath, her sarcasm was actually funny.

"I know I should have called you, I suck."

"That you do."

"Oh thanks a lot." I said as I laughed again.

"So you can laugh, that is cool."

I rolled my eyes and laid back on my bed. "I do laugh, yes . . . when something is funny."

Wendy sat there and I could hear her breathing and I closed my eyes as I imagined her lips again . . . those damn lips of hers . . . damn it. Then she spoke again.

"Jude?" she said.

"Yes Wendy."

"I want to see you again."

"I cannot imagine why."

Wendy laughed. "You can't be that stupid."

I smiled. "I don't know why you think that I am a good idea."

"Val told me . . ."

"Please don't talk about her okay?" I asked her. She stopped and I could hear her breathing again.

"Sorry."

"She was my friend and I cannot help but talk about her when talking to you." she said.

"I am asking you to stop." I said.

"Okay." she said and I once again clinched my fist and knocked it against my forehead as I sat up and said the last thing I thought I would.

"We should go out again Wendy."

I heard her light up as she spoke to me. "Really?"

"Yes, really." I said.

"Look out your window." she said.

I stood up and walked to my window, I pushed the curtain aside and she stood by her car and waved at me.

"You creep me out." I said.

She laughed and lowered her phone and hung up. I sighed and placed my phone in my pocket knowing this was a suck idea, but she is here and I said it . . . so now what?

I stepped outside and she stood there looking so good that if old Jude was present, you know the one before all the suicide shit, I would have grabbed her and thrown her in the backseat . . . but this is Wendy and she is not just some random chick. I placed my hands in my pockets and walked up to her and she smiled.

"Can I at least drive?" I asked her and she threw me the keys and I opened her door and she got in all happy and in my opinion for absolutely no reason.

I started up the car and looked over at her.

"Disastrous date part two, coming right up." I said and Wendy laughed, making me feel less awkward and more normal than I should right now.

We drove for awhile and instead of thinking about a destination I just kind of settled into just going and not doing. I did glance over at Wendy a few times, who had taken her shoes off and thrown her feet out the window. She leaned back on her seat, wind blowing her top open a little and I swerved and she laughed and looked at me.

"I would not be opposed to a kiss." she said to me.

I raised my eyebrows and looked at her again.

"While we are driving?" I asked her.

"Why not?" she asked as she slid over and touched my leg causing me to swerve again. She leaned up into my ear and whispered.

"I want you."

I sighed and my heartbeat sped up. I looked at her and she touched my face and the next thing I knew she had her lips pressed against mine. I moaned at her mouth and it was then that the car rocked and we both looked forward, Wendy yelling out and me trying like hell to stomp on the brakes, the car lost control and we hit the ditch and then rolled into the field. The car came to a stop and I quickly raised my hand to my head and it felt wet, I lowered my hand and saw blood and Wendy started to feel every part of me.

"Oh my GOD! are you okay? . . . oh no Jude, you are bleeding!"

"I'm fine . . . I am."

She quickly pulled out her phone and dialed 911 and I stumbled out of the car and held onto the hood.

"Oh look at this, I am so sorry." I said.

Wendy waved her hand at me and told the operator where to find us and I sighed, as once again the date from hell continued

Then I dropped and Wendy screamed as I passed out.

*　　*　　*

I woke up in a white room hooked up to an IV.

"Mr. Franklin you and Ms. Brandsworth got in a wreck, but you both should be out of here in an hour, you hit your head on the dashboard." The young hot doctor told me.

"We were kissing . . ."

"That is what she said."

I looked at her and then next to me and saw Wendy smiling as if she was embarrassed.

"I think you should stay away from me." I said.

"Absolutely not." Wendy said.

"Well, lets see . . . I wrecked your car, great date."

"Seriously? I don't care about the car."

I laughed and then narrowed my eyes as a slight pain welled up in my head.

"Okay . . . laughing, not so good."

Wendy laughed and then she touched my hair and I looked at her face again, I cannot blame it on beer or memory this time, it was just her and she looked beautiful.

Then she leaned up and with one slow motion she kissed me, softer than anyone ever had before and the pain started to fade in my head. I waited, I was sure that I would start to flashback to something about Val, it seemed inevitable that I would ruin the moment but as she kissed me and then started to play with my hair, I became engulfed in only thoughts of her. I started to pull her on top of me and she let me.

"I am sorry." I whispered to her.

"Show me." she whispered back and I did the best that I knew how.

CHAPTER TWELVE

Heart vs Body

We got discharged at eight and I happily let Wendy drive her car to her house.

We pulled into my driveway with it sputtering and spitting out white smoke. I kissed her goodbye and felt the need to say I was sorry again, but did not. I felt like we had a moment in the hospital that told her all the apologies I would need to give to her.

"Jude, where have you been?" My mom asked as I walked in the house.

"Well, if you must know, I was making out and crashed a car." I told her letting my Texas voice take over.

"What?" she said in a panic as she walked to me and touched the bandage on my head.

"I am fine." I told her.

"Let me see that!" my Mom said.

"It's fine . . . I am fine." I said to her.

"Why didn't you call me?"

"I was having sex."

My Mom stepped back from me. "Jude David Franklin."

"You asked me."

"Don't do that."

"Sex? Too late."

"Don't be smart, you call me if you have something like that happen."

"I'm sorry." I said, feeling like a broken record.

"You understand me?" she asked.

"Yes, ma'am."

I walked to my room and my landline rang and it was Wendy.

"Everything okay?" Wendy asked

"Sure"

"Is your Mom mad?"

"What do you think?" I asked her.

"I would think yes." she said.

"Well, I distracted her from the injury, I told her we had sex."

"Jude!"

"I did."

"I cannot believe you did that." Wendy said completely shocked.

"I tell her everything."

"I will never be able to meet her now."

"She will like you a lot."

"You think?"

"I know." I said as assumingly as I could to her.

"Well, I gotta go. Time to explain the car to Mom."

"Good luck." I said. "Why don't you come over after you tell her?"

"Thanks, I need it . . . . and I will, if you want me to."

"I do." I said.

I hung up before she did and walked out to our living room.

"Mom, Joey, Wendy is coming over in a little bit, so be nice." I told them as I sat down.

"Sure, son." Mom answered.

"Whatever." Joey said but that was no shock to me, ever since Dad went to war.

"I really hope you like her, Momma." I said acting like Joey never said anything.

"We will see." Mom said with a smile.

I relaxed the best that I could with a headache lingering and then I jumped up when I heard her car pull up a good three hours after she had dropped me off.

The door bell rang and I ran to the door more like a girl than a guy would, Joey and Mom laughed. I opened the door pulling Wendy into a hug and kissing her lightly.

"Hi." I greeted her with a smile.

I turned to my mom and brother with my arm still around Wendy.

"Mom, Joey, this is Wendy." My face lit up.

Only Mom stood up, I took my arm off of Wendy so Mom could greet her.

Mom shook her hand as I expected her too and Wendy glanced at me.

"Dear, you'll have to forgive my youngest son over there, he hasn't been the same since my husband Josh went to war." My mom told Wendy with a sad look on her face.

"Oh, Mrs. Franklin, how sad for you and your family to have to live like this." Wendy told my mom feeling bad.

"Oh he does this to himself, I would know." I told them sourly.

"Wendy, call me, Lori." Mom smiled acting like I didn't bad mouth my brother.

"Okay."

I walked Wendy to a chair and sat next to her, who was next to Joey.

"Hi, you must be Joey, I am Wendy." Wendy told my brother with a smile.

"Hey, Wendy you seem nice so I'll spare us all." Joey said getting up and walking away.

After about an hour we decided to take a walk and ended up at Sunset Beach. I stopped as I watched the water lapping the shore. Wendy was staring at me and I finally turned to her and grinned.

"Listen Wendy."

"I know what you are going to say Jude."

"What do you think I am going to say."

"That you can't do this."

I took a breath and looked at the water again."

"Well, that is pessimistic."

Wendy shrugged her shoulders and I turned back to her.

"I was not going to say that exactly."

"But close to it, right?" she said.

"No, not really. I was going to say this is your opportunity to walk."

"What?" Wendy said as she looked at me the wind blew her hair back making her look more like a model on the cover of some magazine than a girl who would be this insecure.

"Wendy, I am like a broken toy."

Wendy smiled and touched my face. "I like fixing things."

I would have normally been annoyed by someone saying that but for some reason her words made me feel better.

"I have no idea if I can do this right for you."

"I am not asking anything of you Jude." she said.

"I have to be the worst potential boyfriend in the history of boyfriends."

"Oh potential boyfriend, huh?" Wendy asked me as she smiled.

"Well, yeah . . . I mean, if you want, I mean."

"I want." she said as she moved closer to me and instead of getting all crazy I just let her hug me. I needed it and I believe that she did too.

"Listen, let me feed you." I said.

"Are you sure that it will not blow up?" she asked me and I laughed.

"I have to say it is a 50/50, so you will just have to take your chances.

We started to walk and found one of my favorite spots to eat and I stepped up to the door and smiled.

"Table for two." I said.

The host smiled and walked us to our table and the place looked empty.

"Are you sure that the food is okay here?" Wendy asked me.

"Of course, it is just a slow night."

Wendy laughed. "Or everyone is sick from eating here."

"How about we think positive?" I said as I laughed at her.

*   *   *

I pulled out the chair for her.

"Here you go." I said with a smile.

"Why, thank you, Jude." Wendy said blushing.

"You're welcome." I replied.

"Do you have your ID?" I asked with a wink.

"Jude David, now why would I have that?" She asked with a laugh.

"Waiter, we'd like some wine!!" I yelled.

"Okay, Sir, can I see some ID?" She asked.

"Sure, here's mine." I said trying to be friendly.

"Do you like red or white, Sir?" He asked kissing my ass, as he should . . . I'm paying.

"Red." I said.

"And your lady?" She asked.

"Ask her." I told her with a laugh.

"White, thank you." She smiled.

"Your welcome, I'll be back." She said as she walked away.

I looked at Wendy who was getting prettier by the moment, I swear. In fact, I should have seen it all along, but I think I was ignoring it. The waiter returned with the wine and I smiled as she lifted hers to her mouth and I watched her.

"Tell me something Jude."

"What?"

"Do you ever think about marriage?"

I choked on my drink so badly the waiter came running and felt the need to jerk me up out of my seat and gave me the Heimlich. I smacked at her and shook my head, grabbing the napkin and covering my mouth.

"Seriously?" I asked her and she sat there looking completely deflated.

The waiter left us and I rolled my eyes and sat back down.

"I didn't mean us." she said to me.

"I didn't mean to choke; it just came out of left field."

"I am a girl."

"That you are." I said and as the hurtful look came over her face I leaned forward and had to make a save.

"And a beautiful one at that." I whispered.

She grinned, allowing me to save the moment from her craziness.

"Yes." I said and she looked at me.

"Yes what?"

"I thought about marriage, once." I added.

"Oh . . ." she said, letting her words trail off.

"Listen, Wendy. Val was something, I mean . . . to me, there was a time that she was everything, I would be lying if I said that marriage did not cross my mind."

"I hear you."

"But . . . Val is not here, this is you and me and not me and Val tonight."

Wendy watched my face almost as if she expected me to add another "but" in there, but I didn't have any. In fact all I felt was happy, and happy was so needed, even if it meant me saying something that might not be true. Val was always with me and I had a bad feeling that she would never really leave.

I know that the perfect dude move at that point would have been to kiss her hand, or better yet her lips. Wendy looked at me as if she wanted that but I sat there and the waiter came back and helped me by interrupting the moment.

"Sir, dinner is ready." The waiter said.

After we ate, I paid the bill and we walked, Wendy placed her hand into mine and I let her although I still had my doubts about everything. But this is it. I told her it was her and me, and I feel obligated to make that happen. We stepped up to her house and I smiled as she turned to me.

"I am alone tonight." she said.

"Oh . . . is that an invitation?" I asked her.

She laughed.

"Listen, I am not like this normally. I would not have slept with someone so fast, but we did and now . . ." she stopped, feeling like she was saying too much.

"I want to come in." I said as I looked at her and grinned.

"You do?" she asked me.

"Well . . . yeah? I mean come on." I said as I laughed.

She smiled and we walked into her house and I looked around. She left me for a moment and came back with two ice waters and I grinned.

"Trying to sober up?" I asked her.

"Well, I don't want this to be a situation where you think that I took advantage of you."

I had to laugh and I took the water and set it down. I pulled her to me.

"How can the willing be taken advantage of?" I asked her.

We lowered to the floor and I kissed her and then she rolled me onto my back and looked down at me.

I smiled and touched her hair as she leaned in and then memory snuck up on me again and I let it, although I should not have . . . because it is so unfair to Wendy.

*   *   *

"I'll give you the ring if it never touches a finger again." Mr. V. said handing me Val's ring.

"I swear on Val's dead body that I will wear this around my neck in reminder that she was my only true love." I vowed looking Mr. V. in the eyes.

"Then we have a deal son." Mr. V. smiled.

"You have no idea what this means to me, Sir." I told him putting the ring on the chain with Dad's dog-tag.

"Yes, I do Jude. I was you, 18 years ago." Mr. V. said with a sad look in his eyes.

*   *   *

I broke the kiss and sat up, feeling the ring on the chain around my neck and stood up quickly. Wendy watched me as I adjusted my shirt and headed for the door.

"Are you okay Jude."

I looked back at her and nodded.

"I'm fine, I need to go. The wine is messing with my stomach." I lied, I had too . . . Val was in my head, messing with my mind and leaning heavy on my heart.

CHAPTER THIRTEEN

Worst Nightmare

I quickly understood what was going on as I walked in the house.

"I don't get it, Joey!!" My mom yelled.

"What don't you get Mom? I miss Dad and Jude is not around, it's not like I can talk to you, I need a guy not a mom who acts like she gets it, when you don't!!" Joey yelled back.

"It's okay to miss your dad, but it's not okay to do drugs!!" Mom told him.

"Don't tell me what I can and can't do." Joey said coldly, pushing passed his Mom.

"I can and will, I'm your mother!!" She said pulling him back to face her.

"Don't touch me, bitch!!" Joey yelled slapping her on the face so hard she fell to the ground.

"You don't talk to Mom like that. And you never hit her." I said coming up behind him and pinning him to the ground so he couldn't hurt her.

"Look who came to join the party." He laughed mocking me.

My hands started to shake and sweat.

"Awe, baby losing his grab? That's too bad, never pin a druggy!!" He yelled as he pulled himself out of my hold and stood up.

He stepped closer and the next thing I knew I heard a crack and everything went black.

I woke up to bright lights and an IV beeping.

I heard foot steps, hard foot steps. I knew who it was without even looking.

"Daddy?" I asked in a low tone.

"Yes, son, it's me, I'm here and it will all be okay." My dad said in the same voice.

"Where's Mom? Where's Joey?" I asked all at once.

"Mom went to get a snack and Joey is hiding in the hallway, he'll come in later, you two need to talk. The doctor came in and got an X-ray, son it doesn't look good." Dad's eyes went cold at the last word.

"Dad, what is it? What's wrong with me?" I asked with tears in my eyes.

"We all need to hear this as a family, the doctor told me when your Mom left." Dad told me.

"Well, in the mean time, Joey, you jackass . . . get in here." I called weakly into the hallway.

Joey slowly walked in with his head down and his hands behind his back.

"Oh, Jude I'm so sorry, you need to help me . . . . I'M YOUR BROTHER, HELP ME." Joey started out low and then yelled.

Next thing I knew Jack Rush, the man that is working on Val's case, came in.

"Well, well, well, you Franklin's are a handful." Rush said in a cold tone, pulling a bottle out and spitting in it. I turned away. People that dip, gross me out, it's not classy. This is California not Oklahoma.

"What's going on?" I asked looking around at the hard faces in my room.

"Ask your pussy brother." Rush said, pushing him forward.

"I . . . . didn't . . . . I . . . . wasn't." Joey started to say, but he couldn't get it out.

"TELL ME WHAT YOU DID COWARD!!!" I yelled not knowing where it came from, I just wanted to yell.

"I . . . . broke . . . . it." Joey said in a baby voice, crying.

"WHAT DID YOU BREAK?" I asked, shaking.

"Your back . . . . it's gone." Joey said with no feeling as he fell to the ground.

"Gone . . . . done . . . . finished?" I asked myself.

"YOU ASSHOLE, LEAVE . . . I NEED TO TALK WITH MY BROTHER ALONE." I yelled at Rush.

"You need to leave too Dad go find Mom." Joey spoke for me.

"I'll be outside if you need me, boy." Rush said, looking me in the eyes.

I nodded and then we were alone man to man, brother to brother.

"I just lost the love of my life and a baby I will never know. I was starting to feel somewhat normal, then YOU HAD TO FUCK IT ALL UP, AND YOU KNOW WHAT?" I yelled in his face. "I DON'T BELIEVE YOU, YOU WANTED TO BE ME, YOU ARE JUST TRYING TO HAVE THE BETTER LIFE, FUCK YOU I CAN WALK." I yelled as I got up to walk and fell to the ground.

I felt him pick me up and hold me like a baby, I wanted for him to put me in bed, but he just stayed on the ground sobbing.

"I love you brother, I do. I'll hate myself forever because I did fuck up your life, you're right. I think jail is the only thing for me now." He cried.

"I think you're right, you need to go to jail and get clean, it could be someone's life next." I said coldly.

"I know." Was all he could say.

"Do you still believe you can walk?" He asked.

"No but I don't want Mom to hear it from you, I'll ask Dad to get the doctor. Put me in bed." I told him, still mad.

"Rush, we are done here but I think my mom has the right to see her son before jail." I told him as he walked in.

Joey sat in a chair next to my bed.

Dad and Mom walked in my room.

I looked up through teary eyes and tried to speak, but no words came to me.

"We will beat this, as a family." Mom vowed as she kissed my forehead, I blushed.

Mom walked over to Joey.

"I'm you're son, how could you call the cops?" Joey cried.

"You have done too much to this family; I won't let you hurt us anymore." Mom said as she walked away.

Just then, the doctor walked into my room.

"Hello, Mr. Franklin good to see you again, wish it was on better terms."

I need to thank the doctor later for bringing up my last trip, not.

"Again?" My Dad asked.

"I just want to hear what's wrong with me." I said dancing around the topic.

"Well, Jude your brother broke your back when he stepped on it. Your X-ray looked pretty bad, I'm sorry to tell you there is nothing we can do. You will never be able to walk again, I'm so sorry." The doctor said with no feeling and walked out of my room.

Rush came in and said, "It's time to go son."

"Jude! Jude!" Joey cried out as he was pulled out of my room. "I'm so sorry!" was the last thing I heard before the door closed and he was gone.

I looked at my Mom and my Dad, I knew they loved me, but could I still love myself after this?

I looked up as Wendy pushed past a nurse who was trying to stop her from entering the room. She stopped and had the worst look on her face as she saw me in the hospital bed with an IV hanging out of my arm.

"Oh my God . . . Jude, what happened?" she asked me, half out of breath. I looked at my Mom and she turned to Wendy.

"Jude had an accident, he will be okay." she said.

I clinched my fists and stared at her and then looked at Wendy.

"I am NOT OKAY!" I yelled out as the tears came, all the ones that had been held back since Val died and all the ones that were needed now.

"Oh honey." My Mom said and I pushed her away as she leaned into me.

"Just leave . . . seriously . . . leave me alone."

My dad and my mom listened to me and left the room. Wendy stood there looking like she had been hit by a train.

"Jude."

"That meant you too Wendy." I said as I stared her down.

"Please, tell me what is wrong." she said and I looked up to her.

"I can't walk Wendy, I will never walk . . . okay?" I said.

"What?"

"Yes . . . my brother Joey broke my back, he is a drug addict and he was fighting with my Mom and I tried to stop him."

"Oh god."

"Don't do that."

Wendy looked at me. "Do what?"

"Sound all sad for me, just leave."

Wendy took a step closer to me.

"I mean it Wendy, this is me telling you to get out of here."

Wendy took another step towards me.

"No." she said quietly.

"I so don't want you here."

Wendy stepped closer. "You need me Jude."

"I don't." I said as my heartbeat faster in my chest and my breathing became shallow.

"Jude . . . please . . . let me." she said as she was suddenly holding me and I tried to push her away but she held on like she was never going to let me go.

"Wendy . . ." I tried to say and she kissed me and I started to cry and she laid down in the bed next to me and held my hand and we said nothing, we didn't need to.

*   *   *

I woke up to the lights on and my mother looking over at us.

"I called Wendy's mom, told her that she was here. I see why you think she is something special, I believe that she is." My mom said quietly so Wendy wouldn't wake.

"Yeah, she is. Thanks Mom, I know this is hard on you." I told her stroking Wendy's hair as I talked.

"Oh honey it's not a big deal, you're hurting worse than me. You need Wendy. She can stay as long as she wants." Mom said trying to be happy for me.

"Thanks." I said as I glanced at Wendy who was sleeping.

"Jude, do you love her?" My Mom asked me and something in me wanted to say yes but I just looked at my Mom and grinned.

"I like her a lot."

"Well that is good."

"For me . . . not so much for her."

"Why do you say that?" My Mom said as she touched my hair.

"Because who would want me now?" I asked her.

"Jude, don't talk like that."

I glanced at Wendy and sighed.

"If I wasn't messed up enough for her before, I certainly am now."

"Jude David . . . stop talking like that. I think it is wonderful that she came to see you."

"Yeah, she just loves broken things."

My Mom sighed and left us alone and I touched Wendy's face and hoped that I was what she needed, because I suddenly needed her.

Chapter Fourteen

Pride is Pride no matter
how you spin it

Wendy sat in the chair next to my bed watching *Regis and Kelly*, giving me my space as we waited for Mom and Dad to come back from a coffee run. I use to like the quiet, to allow me to think. But, the mind is a trap for me now. Be with Wendy, let Wendy go, forget Val, hold on to Val. I try to look at random things in the room and and just zone out, I wished it worked.

"Damn it . . . ."

Wendy turned her head at the sound of my voice, I sighed, I didn't want her to hear me.

"Does it hurt?"

I shook my head. I wasn't talking about that kind of pain. It would be much easier if I was.

"Jude, you aren't invincible, no one is."

I slowly rolled on my side, a nurse walked in to fill my IV.

"Mr. Franklin, it's not good to be on your side, here let me help you so you don't hurt yourself."

"It's Jude and no, I'm fine, thanks, the view was giving me a headache."

"Oh I can shut the blinds."

"That won't help, just leave please."

The nurse gave me a smile but looked like she wanted to give me the evil eye before she walked away.

Wendy walked over to my bed and sat down.

"Wendy . . . . listen I know you are trying to help but the best way to help is to go back to your chair. I'm unpredictable right now."

Wendy sat up straighter and turned her body to face me.

"I happen to like unpredictable . . . ."

"I forgot for a minute that you like what you shouldn't. What, did your dad keep you on a chain and this is your way of getting back at him?"

"I mean if it's role play that you're into . . . ."

I laughed, I actually laughed for the first time since I've been in this fucked up situation. Wendy moved her lips closer to mine.

"I'm not running Jude, no matter hard you try. It will never work."

Her lips touched mine and she almost fell on top of me, catching herself by planting her hands firmly on the mattress. When Wendy kisses me I always know where we are heading but my body did not seem to want to go where my mind did.

"Umm Wendy?"

"Yes?"

God how can I do this? It's like every man's worse nightmare, oh wait, it can't get any worse than when I already woke up. Alright let's try again . . . . I pushed my body harder with hers, hello? Is anyone home?

"Yup, sorry it's not happenin'."

"That's okay Jude, this is a hard time for you, maybe that's it."

I turned red and banged my head on the pillow.

"Sorry, that was worded wrong . . . ."

"Yeah, it sure was . . . . this is not just a glitch Wendy, I think I will never be able to have sex."

Wendy lowered her herself, putting her arm around me. I wanted to push her away but for some odd reason I didn't and that in itself is a glitch. I think we must have drifted to sleep because two coffees were on the nightstand next to my bed when I opened my eyes. I then focused in on my Dad, who must have come in as I slept.

"Oh thank God, I've missed you."

"Awe, son you don't know how much that means to me."

"Oh yeah, I've missed you too Dad . . . ."

"Jude, I think that you should kick the coffee for awhile."

"And I think you're crazy, coffee is like my anti-depressant."

See, this is way I love my Dad, he laughed, my Mom would have taken it to heart.

"So, son, you've done pretty good."

Dad eyed Wendy with a smile.

"Oh, well, I really don't know what I'm going to do about that."

"I know what you're thinking about doing."

"Dad . . . . I've been meaning to talk to you about that."

My Dad waited for me to say something.

"I . . . . Oh God Dad I really didn't want to talk to you about this but I don't have any friends to turn to . . . . I can't get it up."

"Oh . . . ."

Yeah, that's what I would say too.

"Well, son, there are options . . . ."

"Yeah, I've watched a lot of ESPN they need to stop thinking just old men watch Sports Center."

Sometimes when I get nervous I make jokes to lighten the mood in this case it didn't work that well.

"Jude David, listen I will talk to Dr. Dallas and we'll get on meds, I know pride can get in the way but Jude if she likes you it shouldn't change anything."

This made everything so real to me, before when I was talking to Wendy it was like if I kept trying it would work but now that I was really talking about it, I knew it was true, not just a 'Oh try again tomorrow' type of thing. I needed to yell.

"Damn it Dad, you don't get it, I CAN'T WALK AND NOW I CAN'T HAVE SEX."

I looked next to me and saw that Wendy's eyes were wide open.

"Go Wendy, you don't have to see this . . . ."

"Oh but I do Jude, go on."

"I will go see Dr. Dallas, nice to meet you Wendy."

With that, my Dad walked out of my room and shut the door behind him.

"It's not the end of the world Jude."

"Get out of my face."

"You don't mean that . . . ."

"I do, more than you will never know."

I couldn't walk away and I couldn't make Wendy leave. This is unfortunate because I had nothing to say and I wasn't going to listen to what she had to say.

Wendy sighed and put her arm around me this time I shook it off me.

"Okay, Jude I'm not one of those girls you can just toss aside. So I'm going to be frank with you, we have something if you can't act like we do, then call me when you can."

I let the silence continue not wanting to respond to her because I just wasn't ready to say what she wanted to hear. I couldn't tell her that I needed her, that's like saying 'I love you' in my book. With Val, a lot of it was about sex. I'm not saying it was like a Drake type of thing, I think we did love each other but let's face it, we were just teenagers. Wendy reached out to me and I closed my eyes as her warm hand caressed my face. I felt less tense when we were touching and started to lower my wall as much as I could, baby steps.

Wendy may have not known it at the time but it was a big step for me, to let her touch me . . . calm me down, when I didn't even know that I could.

"Where did the name Wendy come from?" I asked her, wanting to be nice.

"My Grandpa's name is Wendell, what about you?"

"Jude is just Jude, I don't know."

"I think it's Catholic . . . ."

"My Grandmother was one I bet that's why."

"We all need something to believe in . . . ."

We all do need something to believe in, no matter what I've done in my life I always counted on my Dad, it was only when he went to war that I started to lose faith in his point of view. Maybe Dad is right, I'm not sure what me and Wendy are but I do know that she believes in me just as much as my Dad does and I can't say that about a lot of people.

As if to read my mind Wendy spoke up. "I think you should tell your Dad that you're sorry."

I knew that it was the right thing to do but I wanted to do it on my terms not because Wendy told me to. It's like being little and your parents tell you to say thank you after someone does something for you; it makes you not want to say it even more.

"See, Wendy I can't, I'm not a liar."

Wendy touched my face and had a dead lock on my eyes. I wanted to turn away but it was like time stopped and I couldn't move no matter how hard I tried. That's a lie itself, you want to say sorry but you're not man enough. Will you have the balls to say that, tough guy?

"No . . . ."

That's what I thought . . . . my inner voice said.

"Well you're wrong, I mean . . . . guess I'm wrong." I said out loud, to myself.

"What was that Jude?"

"Nothing."

Just fighting with yourself, go ahead, tell her that and see if she isn't running then. My inner voice said with spite.

"She swore . . . . I believe her." I muttered. I knew Wendy didn't know what I was talking about.

You should say you want to believe her, ha, liar again . . . . my inner voice said as it laughed at me.

"Jude I think they need to stop giving you so much Morphine . . . ." Wendy said.

Yup, that's it alright . . . . my inner voice said again.

"Stop it." I said as I started to get irritated.

Tell the truth . . . . my inner voice said.

"I will not . . . ." I yelled out.

Oh Wendy if you think Val was crazy, wait till you see the real Jude. I held my head everything was spinning now from the stress of the fight with my inner self. Wendy pressed the button behind my bed.

"Yes?"

"Is it normal for people to talk to themselves when on Morphine?"

"Who are you speaking of?"

"Jude Franklin." Wendy said as she stared at me.

"Oh dear we will be right there, but don't worry he'll be fine."

Things started to get blurry after that, maybe I was going crazy. I just remember Dr. Dallas and a lot of nurses came in my room and then I think I blacked out to Wendy's voice telling me it would be okay.

CHAPTER FIFTEEN

Preview

I woke up alone and I was happy. I mean, all I remember was a meltdown, and in front of Wendy no less. I sighed and looked over at the IV and noticed that it was no longer in my arm and I sat up and looked around the room. This was the hospital right? Oh shit, I hope I am not in some messed up coma or some shit, then the door opened and the nurse walked in and grinned at me as I waited for her to turn into a dragon or something . . . I mean, that is what happens when you are crazy right? Things transform. The nurse walked up to my bed and smiled.

"You leave today Jude." she said and I was relieved, as long as this is real.

Then my dad stepped in and I tried to move and my damn legs would not and the reality set in, that I was awake, this is real and now I have to face it and my life.

"Jude, you get to come home today son." my dad said as he tried to help me and I swiped my hand at him, feeling a little defiant.

"Let me do this." I said as I pulled on one leg and then the other, I started to tip and my Dad caught me and I did grin at him, I should say thank you, but I can't.

We drove home after a struggle to get into the car . . . not that it could not have been easy, but I made it as hard as I could by trying to do it all myself. When my Dad rolled me into the house my Mom came running to me and giving me kisses. I narrowed my eyes and then allowed her to finish up her unneeded affection towards me.

"I want to go to my room." I said.

"Well, Jude." My Mom said as she looked at my Dad. I looked at both of them and shook my head.

"What?"

"Honey . . . we moved you downstairs, to be easier."

"What?" I said as I started to get mad.

"Honey . . . we have no easy way to get you up there."

"Screw that." I rolled myself to the bottom of the stairs and looked up. It was a daunting task, but I was determined. I started to pull myself out of the chair and I fell, my Mom tried to run to me but my Dad shook his head and held her arm. I struggled with the first step and then pushed myself onto my back and covered my face with my hands.

"Jude . . . son." my dad said.

I uncovered my face and looked at him.

"Fine . . . take me to my new room." I said, so not ready to talk about any of this shit . . . as if anyone would be.

I sat in my chair in my new room, which was actually My dad's study. I looked around and saw everything, my bed, my dresser all of my things. I turned as my Dad walked in and looked at me.

"Son."

"What?" I said as I rubbed the inside of my palm.

"Your mom has enrolled you in a new school."

"What?"

"Son, it will help you."

"Who said I needed help."

My dad did not dignify that with an answer. He walked to my door and then turned back to me.

"You start tomorrow." he said and with that the decision had been made whether I liked it or not.

*   *   *

"This is Jude, Jude welcome, tell us your story." The teacher said.

They were all in high-class wheelchairs that Mommy and Daddy got them so they would feel better. Not me, not yet anyway.

"I'm Jude Franklin, I have a vertebral body compression fracture and the doctors say I'll never walk again. My brother, Joey is a druggie and when my mom found out she lost it and he hit her, I stepped in and he got me down on the ground and stepped on my back." I said with tears in my eyes.

"Well, Jude we all have had a hard life that has brought us all here today." The teacher said in a sad tone like everyone should feel bad for us.

I'm just trying to live my life the best way I can, I want to be treated just like anyone else. I understand why I have to be here but I wish I didn't have to.

"Okay today we are learning how to go from our wheelchairs to a normal sitting chair. Some of you who have been here a long time have mastered this, so for you guys I want you to go outside and try to get up curbs." The teacher told all of us, I knew he was going to keep an eye on me today.

I tried the first time to move from the wheelchair and fell. The teacher said I should use my arms for everything in my new body. As other kids did harder things, he had me doing push-ups and pull-ups to make my arms less weak and more like the other kids. When I told him that I couldn't do something, he started yelling and told me to go faster.

After about an hour when we were done, I was so tired.

I sat out in front of the school and when I saw Wendy drive up my heart fluttered in my chest to see her again. She got out of the car and walked up to me smiling.

"How was your work-out?" Wendy asked looking at the sweat on my face.

"What are you doing here?"

"Well, manners are not your strong point." Wendy said as she started to push me and I started to roll on my own, forcing her hands off of my chair.

I stopped at the car door and knew I would now need help. Wendy walked up and looked at me, sort of grinning.

"Jude." she said as she stared at me.

"Could you . . ." I started to say.

"Help you?" Wendy said and I nodded.

"I think a please would do it." she added.

"Listen, I could just roll home." I looked at her.

"Right . . . it is blocks from here."

"Watch me." I said as I started to roll away from her.

"Jude Franklin!" she yelled at me.

I kept on going, ignoring her and then suddenly she ran up behind and flipped my brakes on and I jerked in my chair. She stepped around in front of me and crossed her arms on her chest.

"You are an asshole." she said.

"Then let me go do asshole stuff." I said.

She smiled and held back a laugh.

"Is it impossible for you to say thank you, or please?" she said to me.

"I can do things on my own."

Wendy sighed and knelt down to one knee and looked at me.

"Jude, there is nothing wrong with accepting kindness."

I stared at her and had to hear her kind words. This was kindness, from a pretty and kind girl and it was either be an asshole or allow her to help me.

"Please." I muttered under my breath.

"What?" she said as she leaned forward.

"You heard me." I said.

Wendy smiled as she undid the brake and started to roll me back to the car. She got me in much easier than I expected her too and without conversation we drove to my house and she stopped the car and I glanced at her.

"Jude." she said in a soft voice. I looked at her face and then she kissed me as I tried to move back from her and then something beautiful happened . . . . I started to enjoy it.

I rolled to my room, thinking about that kiss. There was something about how I felt when she leaned away; I didn't want it to end.

When I was with Jenna my mind couldn't touch me and that's why I liked it. When I was with Val I always felt like I was along for the ride, playing the lead role in her show, which used to make me feel needed but in the back of my mind I always knew one day I wasn't going to be needed anymore. It wasn't a need for support; it was more filling a sexual hole. It wasn't like that with Wendy; well it was at first I won't lie. No matter what I do she supports me and I I know that is a scary situation as well because one day she could get sick of my shit. But, I think Wendy needs support too and I think that's the main difference. Wendy pushes me, she doesn't buy the bullshit, she knows that there is something more to me she wants to uncover to help me in the long run. It isn't about her, with Val it always was. I knew I needed to do something soon or I may regret it for the rest of my life. At least if I put myself out there I'd know that I gave it my all.

CHAPTER SIXTEEN

No more Mr. Asshole

I picked up my phone, my heart started pounding and my room felt suddenly hotter than normal. I wasn't use to feeling like this when I called a girl but I knew what I was about to say would not be easy.

"I'm an asshole . . . ."

Wendy laughed.

"Hi asshole, I'm Wendy."

Okay I guess I set myself up for that one, stay focused Jude.

"Ha ha, real funny. Listen I'm an asshole. I'm sure I won't be the last to say that and I sure as hell am not the first. But I want to try to kick that shit to the curb it may not happen right a way but old habits die hard. I guess what I'm trying to say is, I want to give us a shot."

That wasn't as hard as I feared. This was the easy part and if she didn't like what she heard it's her lost.

"Wow, I got to say Jude, I was shocked you even called at all. You know, given your history of kiss-and-run. I guess I'm a really good kisser."

I was happy she didn't make a big deal of it. I mean we knew it was a big deal but there's no need to act like it was. I may be making a change but I'm not ready to let go of the clutch.

"Maybe I'll just let you think it's you so I can get another date, a real one, with the real Jude."

"Is this you asking me out?"

"I think it is, wear something hot . . . ."

I hit 'end' and smiled to myself.

I rolled out of the room and went to the beach it wasn't easy pushing myself in the sand but I didn't want to ask for help. I would build more muscle if I did it on my own. I sat in me and Val's spot and closed my eyes. I imagined her sprit floating in thin air, I never really thought about what heaven would look like so I couldn't imagine it clearly.

"Val, I love you, I always will but it's time for me to let you go. You wanted me to move on and I'm trying but I can't if you are always in the back of my mind."

I talked in a low voice hoping no one would hear me. I knew it would take time to truly move on but each day it would get easier.

I looked down at the ring around my neck. I wanted to toss it in the water but I didn't know if I could. I swore on Val's life to Mr. V . . . . it feels wrong. I broke the chain and the ring and dog tag fell in the sand. I bent down picking up the ring and dog tag; I put the dog tag and broken chain behind my back. The ring felt like a hundred pounds in my hand. Please forgive me, Mr. V., it's a part of letting go. I kissed the ring and tossed it in the water with tears in my eyes. I headed back home before I could change my mind and go franticly digging in the water to find it.

CHAPTER SEVENTEEN

I am not going anywhere

I sat in my room and I swear I had the strongest urge to go back to the beach and dig that ring up, but I sat still, forcing myself to accept it as I should. Time took away my regret and I started to get tired, so I went to bed. I rolled onto my back and the phone rang and I grabbed it, hoping like hell it was Wendy and it was.

"Hello." I said.

"Hi." Wendy said back to me.

"About this date thing." she added and I adjusted on my bed and sat up, feeling a little nervous, hoping she was not about to cancel on me.

"I thought maybe dinner would be nice."

I sighed and moved the phone from one ear to the other.

"Oh . . . that sounds good, where?" I asked her.

"Well, my house, if you want. I actually can cook."

I hesitated and then cleared my throat.

"I thought we could go out." I said to her.

Wendy hesitated too and then spoke. "I thought it would just be easier."

"Oh easier, as in, with me." I said.

"Jude." Wendy said all soft.

"I get it." I said, starting to take it all wrong.

"You get what?" she asked me.

"Are you embarrassed to be out with me now?" I asked her.

"What . . . no Jude!" she said.

"I mean, just be honest."

Wendy sighed. "I am not, and you are teetering on the asshole thing again."

I gripped the phone tightly in my hand.

"I am."

"Yes, Jude . . . you need to work on that, seriously."

"How about you come here for dinner, I can cook too." I said.

"Are you going to poison me?" Wendy asked and I laughed at her.

"I wasn't planning on it, but now that you said it I guess I will have to search the house for cleaners."

We both had a moment of silence and then we busted out laughing, and it felt good . . . better than good, great really.

I spent the whole morning primping, which is the last thing I thought I would be doing. I guess I am just one of those guys who never does much of that and the messy hair thing had worked my whole life. I never had problems getting a girl and now I find myself all nervous and acting as if I need to look awesome. I turned my chair to the mirror and stared at myself. I look hot, don't mind saying it and if Wendy does not jump me, it is 'her bad.' Then I had to swallow that macho shit when the doorbell rang and my insecurity crept in . . . which is also a whole new thing that I am not liking at all.

My Mom walked to the door and I cut her off and stared at her. She smiled, knowing my date was here and did what I hoped she would . . . walked away. I sighed and then I messed my hair up, I mean I had too. I had made it all nice and normal and why? I brushed the front of my shirt and opened the door up to what I can only say was the hottest chick I had seen in a very long time.

Wendy stood there in a red dress; half off her shoulder with her hair braided just over one to one side. I got caught up looking at her boobs and she cleared her throat and I snapped out of it and smiled at her.

"You look amazing." I said.

"You think so?" Wendy said as she smiled and walked in and I kept my eyes on her ass as she turned, then she glanced back at me.

"Pervert." she whispered and I nodded.

"I am thinking awful things right now, that dress is hot."

"Well maybe you will get lucky."

"Damn, I hope so." I muttered as she walked towards our kitchen and smelled the food.

"Wow." Wendy said as she stopped and looked at the table set for two with candles lit. She looked back at me and nodded.

"I am liking this so far." she said to me.

"Well, I hope you like the poison." I joked.

She looked at me and shook her head.

"You poison me I am going to be so pissed."

I laughed and rolled up behind her and pulled her chair out so she could sit down. I took my place across from her and smiled as I lifted the lid from the meal I had prepared. It was a fast food bag, with hamburgers and fries in it. She stared at it and then at me.

I smiled and opened the bag up and took a burger out and handed it to her.

"I thought you said that you cooked."

"First lie and last one . . . promise." I said as I smiled again.

"I could have cooked for us."

"I know but this is easier." I said.

"Jude . . . I didn't mean anything bad, I swear."

"I know, and I am sorry." I said.

Wendy took a bite of her burger and grinned as she inspected it.

"Well, it seems to be okay."

"The poison will not kick in until later; at that point, I have every intention of groping you."

"Oh really?" Wendy said as she laughed and started to cough.

"Well of course . . . look at that dress." I said.

"Is it just the dress?" Wendy asked me.

I looked into her eyes.

"No . . . It's you."

We finished dinner and afterwards I somehow convinced her that going to my room was a good idea. I watched her as she walked around my room and looked at everything then she turned and smiled at me.

"Thank you for dinner, it was good."

"Thank the burger guy."

"I love that place I used to eat there all of the time before I started watching what I ate."

I looked at her grinned.

"You want to make out?"

Wendy nodded and ran to me and we started to kiss like we had not had any sex in years. I had to take a breath and then I touched her face and we kissed again without any words. Then I heard a voice and stopped and looked up to my door, which was now open and the last person I wanted to see was standing there . . . Jenna.

"Oh shit." I muttered.

"Hello." Wendy said as she adjusted her dress, which I had almost ripped off of her.

"Hi . . . who are you?" Jenna asked.

"Ummmm, Wendy."

"Well Wendy, is there a reason you are all over my boyfriend?" she asked.

"Not." I said as I looked at Wendy and she shook her head and started to walk to the door.

"Wendy." I said.

Jenna watched her leave and I sat there, ready to have sex and Wendy gone . . . perfect.

"What the hell?" I asked Jenna.

Jenna smiled.

"Drake says Hi." she said and with that she was gone and I was pissed.

I tried to call Wendy for the next three days and after listening to her phone go to voicemail for the 100th time I started to feel like a creeper and told myself to stop it. It is not like Wendy is the only chick in the world, but for some reason I could not stop thinking about that dress, her lips, the way she smelled to me and most of all her eyes . . . her eyes killed me. They were so soft and pretty and when she looked at me that night I felt her, and it felt awesome to have someone look at me like that again.

I know that I should just stop it, I know that I should go to the bar and drink a beer and try to turn on the Jude charm, but the last time I went I ended up with Jenna and look how that turned out. I had also not talked to my Dad for three days either. After all, he was the one who let Jenna in as he returned home. I know that he didn't know that Wendy was there . . . he was tricked by Jenna and he let her in but it did not change the fact that it messed stuff up big time.

I decided to stop being all girlie about it and maybe going out would be something good. I rolled to the front door and opened it as my Dad walked up behind me.

"I am sorry about the other night."

"No big deal." I said as I rolled out and towards the bar.

I navigated my way up to barstool and tapped on the bar and Drake leaned over and grinned at me.

"You owe me." I said and Drake walked around the bar and handed me a beer and I rolled to a table and said nothing. He walked up, lifted a chair and turned it around, sitting on it and resting his hands on the top of it.

"That Wendy chick is trouble." he said to me.

I set my beer down and looked at him.

"How would you know?" I asked him.

Drake laughed and looked around the bar.

"I can smell whore." he said.

"Don't talk about her like that." I said.

"What? You would think that after Val you would be more careful about who you sleep with."

I slammed my beer down and looked him in the eye.

"I have not slept with her!" I yelled at him and the bar got quiet for a minute.

Drake smiled and shook his head.

"I am just saying . . . rumor . . ."

I interrupted him.

"Rumor is . . . your sister is the whore." I said a little too loud and that is when I spotted Jenna in the back of the bar and I rolled my eyes.

"I am not defending her." Drake said and I laughed. Of course Drake would not defend family . . . I mean he sent her in to sabotage me.

Jenna walked up and took the beer from my hand and drank it then she slapped me across the face and walked out.

I sat there and shook my head, rubbing the side of my face.

"She is also a bitch." Drake said as he stood up and walked away from me.

I sat in the bar and had three more beers before I rolled myself out, too drunk to argue and to dizzy to care about anything. I rolled down the sidewalk and then without warning a car rolled up beside me and I looked over to see Wendy.

I rolled my eyes and continued to move forward.

Wendy rolled down her window.

"You should not drink and roll." she said.

I would have laughed but for some reason I felt angry at the world, I would assume it was the alcohol.

"Jude." Wendy said and then she stopped the car and got out, running up to me and she stopped me from moving. I rolled to the right, then to the left and she stood in my way.

"Could you move?" I asked her.

"Oh, are we back to asshole status?" Wendy asked.

"I am just Jude, Wendy . . . this is me. I sleep with girls and don't call, I say things I do not mean just to see boobs and now I am drunk as, I want to be."

Wendy placed her hands on her hips and stared me down.

"So . . . you don't like me?" she asked.

"I have no idea." I said to her as I refused to look her in the eyes.

"Jude." Wendy said as she leaned down and tried to look in my face.

"You called me and I should have answered, I was mad." she said.

"You should be . . . I had sex with her." I said.

"What?" Wendy asked as she stood up.

"I did . . . I had sex with her and I liked it, then I did not call her." I said.

"Jude!" she yelled at me.

"What? You want me to lie?" I yelled back at her.

"No! I don't!" she yelled back at me.

"Then why are you yelling?" I yelled back at her.

"I don't know!" she yelled at me.

"You are crazy." I said as I tried to move forward then she jumped on my lap and kissed me hard on the mouth and I fell out my chair and rolled on the ground with her and that was the first time Wendy told me, without saying a word . . . that she wanted me, just as I am.

CHAPTER EIGHTEEN

On the outside looking in

My eyes flew open remembering what happen last night, which was a shock to me because I felt like I had just about the worst hangover in history. I could still smell the grass on my body and I looked over to my muddy jeans and let my mind drift.

*   *   *

I broke the kiss with a laugh, got on my knees and let Wendy help me back into my wheelchair.

"Let's get out of here."

"You took the words right out of my mouth."

We got in the car and headed to the open field that we were at on our first 'date'. Wendy took my chair and put it on the grassy ground. I got in my chair and rolled over to the middle on the field, Wendy followed me.

"So . . . ."

That was all Wendy had to say, I slid to the ground and my lips found hers. She knocked me on my back. With each kiss my head was pressed harder into the Earth, but, I didn't really notice at the time. We both stripped at the same time with one look, I ripped open a condom and put it on, hoping my body wouldn't fail me. Wendy and I moulded together perfectly and nothing brought me more joy. This was no longer about pride for me. It was about us and our feelings for each other. Wendy pulled away from me wiping the perspiration off her face.

"Jude . . . . wow."

I pushed her on the ground letting the fact that I'd been having a dry spell consume me. I was careful not to be rough with her, taking breaks here and there. We finally stopped when we were gasping for air. I wrapped my arms around her and she leaned her head on my bare chest. Wendy traced the letters of my tattoo with her finger.

"You really loved her . . . ."

"Yes very much, I remember when we got the tattoos. It was a week after I asked her to marry me . . . ."

I cut myself off, thinking that this might not be the best story to tell Wendy after we just had sex.

"Go on, I can take it . . . ."

"She was so scared but I told her that it was a symbol of our love for each other. Looking back, it's ironic that it too hurt. I tried to bring myself to remove it but I couldn't and I don't think I will ever be able to."

"And that's okay Jude, no one is asking you to forget Val but they are trying to show you that moving on is a good thing. Val will be in your heart forever but that doesn't mean you don't have room for someone else."

I got the feeling that by 'someone else' she meant her and that scared me. I tried to act like she never said that.

"There was something about Val. Girls wanted to be her best friend and every guy wanted to do her. If there was 50 people in the room, she would make you feel like you were the only one there."

"I wish I could take away your pain Jude. No one should have to live like this."

"My pain is with me forever just like she is. Sure I can remove a tattoo but I can't remove the scars on my heart, they may fade over time however they will never truly go away. It's just not FAIR, she left me with all this shit, it would be easier if she just killed me, I'm dying slowly everyday Wendy. Nothing can change that, not a new room, pack of beer, not even my feeling for you. How could she think giving me you would make up for all this if I can't even be with you because I'm an asshole one day and an emotional wreck the next."

"Jude . . . ."

I turned my back to her.

"Jude . . . ."

She wrapped her arms around my waist and kissed me at the base of my neck.

"I don't care."

"Wendy do yourself a favor and wake up."

I didn't know why I was doing this, messing up what was starting to be something really great. I guess I'm just the paranoia pit of relationships.

"No, I know you have a lot to work on but the Jude I saw at your house the other night proved that's it's worth it."

"How am I worth it when I slept with that whore right after I ran out on our date?"

"Things have change since then but Jude Franklin, if you ever cheat on me I swear, sleep with one eye open . . . ."

"I don't roll like that."

Wendy laughed at my pun and kissed me on the cheek.

*   *   *

There was a knock on my door and a turn of the doorknob.

"Jude, it's time for class, get dressed, I'm driving."

"Oh shit, I'd rather take a beating."

"Rough night?"

"In more ways than one."

My Dad walked away so I could get dressed.

"Okay, class today we aren't working on skills, we have a speaker, Ryan Meadows." The teacher (who I later found out is called Scott) told us.

A tan man with long brown hair in a silver wheelchair came in.

"Hey guys, I'm Ryan, I bet you're happy about not doing skills today so I'll talk as long as I can." Ryan said with a laugh.

"At first I was on crutches but then after some time, I saw it was a lot easier to be in my chair. So you guys are in the right place if there's a way to make things easier you need to do it. When you first get in the chair things are hard as they should be, you are starting a new life style. With time it's like brushing your teeth. So don't give up!!" Ryan added with a smile.

Damn this guy is really good at talking to people if I wasn't so pissed about being here, I might even like him.

"May I ask a question, Mr. Meadows?" I asked with my hand up.

"Sure but it's Ryan and this isn't high school you don't have to put your hand up, thanks." Ryan told me.

"You seem all happy about your life, how did you come to terms with it?" I asked Ryan.

"It's kind of a long story, come see me afterwards and I'll tell you." Ryan said getting sad all of a sudden.

"Okay thanks." I told him.

An hour later, after everyone asked Ryan questions, he came and took a 'walk' with me but it wasn't really a walk because we couldn't walk in the first place.

"I'm Ryan Meadows, my parents are Sara and Scott Meadows, when I was five my dad and I got in a car crash that put us both in chairs. When my mom moved out I was 15 and I felt like it was because of me. Being in the chair at such a young age was hard on me. I didn't really fit in, so I took it out on my dad. Dad had just as a hard of a time as me and when I yelled at him, he got very angry. It got bad. Mom tried to stop him from yelling and hitting me. So when he didn't stop, she moved out. If I never yelled at him as much as I did, we would be a family still. I knew I owed it to her to have a good life because she stood up for me when no one could, I was a kid after all." Ryan said with tears in his eyes.

"But why didn't she take you with her?" I asked.

"After she moved she started to drink because she felt bad about everything that happened. Dad and I are fine today because we have both understood that no one made this happen. Last I heard Mom is in A.A. and getting help but I don't care to see her for along time." Ryan said.

"So you have a good life, except for the mom thing, and you want to now make up for your teenage years?" I asked him.

"I guess you could say that." He said with a wink.

I felt like because Ryan had a hard life, maybe he would understand mine, so I decided to open up to him.

"I was in love with a girl named Valerie she seemed like the normal sweet girl that every guy would want, and I had her. About a month ago she killed herself, she was due to have our baby. Val left me a letter saying I was going meet a girl that she sent for me to be with."

"Wow, that's crazy shit." Ryan said, shocked.

"No one was more shocked than me. I have no idea how to move on."

"You move on for you. As for how to, I can't answer that but you can. If you want to, you will find a way." Ryan told me.

"Good point."

"It's not like you have to right away, no one would ever ask that." Ryan added.

"Thanks Ryan, this helped me so much." I told him, giving him a hug.

"You're welcome, just talking to someone that understands helps." Ryan smiled his perfect smile.

"Yeah, and boy do your understand." I said with a laugh.

"Do you want to have a race with me, I'm better than my old man." Ryan stated.

"Sure . . . . on your mark . . . . get set . . . . go!!" I yelled in happiness.

We took off at a fast speed, but because of my old lady chair I knew Ryan would win.

Ryan was ahead of me by a couple of feet and kept looking back at me. "You need to move your hands out a little bit, lean forward if you can and keep your head up." Ryan told me as he showed me what to do.

"Like this?" I asked him.

"Oh Jude that is perfect." Ryan laughed with excitement. Being with Ryan really made me feel like I was hanging with a normal guy, doing normal things. I liked it. It was fun being with him.

I needed a friend and a nice one at that, Drake would never understand the things I told Ryan. I guess that's the line between them and us. Drake, my Mom and Dad, Brice, Carrie and even Wendy, they all can try to understand and feel what I feel but they can't. Now I see, I have been trying to make people understand for all this time and I can never make them understand. If I have a problem I might tell Wendy and but that will be all, if I'm going to have a breakdown I go to Scott or Ryan.

It felt just as good to hear Ryan happy for me as it did to go fast in the chair.

I smiled and said, "Man, I haven't felt this great in weeks!"

"Glad to hear it but I don't know why I'm training you to beat me." Ryan joked.

So there's going to be more? Great maybe I can get out earlier and have fun as I do it. I'm not going to get out of Scott's class. Ryan can't teach me everything but I wish he could. I really really like him.

I called Wendy to come and get me but this time I'm not letting her push me. Ryan says I need to go as much as I can on my own.

"Ryan, this is Wendy." I said as she walked to my side.

"Ryan is Scott's son he has been helping me today." I told her.

"Oh Ryan it's nice to meet you, you're dad has been so good to Jude." Wendy said with a smile as she shook his hand.

"Well I'm glad he's good to some people." Ryan laughed.

"I'll be in touch man." I told him slapping his hand to mine as I passed.

We got in the car and I told Wendy we should go to the beach bar so I could tell her about my day.

"Two cokes please."

Wendy looked shocked I didn't want a beer.

"What? I'm not an alcoholic."

I felt bad joking about that after what happened with Sara, Ryan's mom.

"So, Ryan seems nice."

"Yeah, he's great it's like when I'm hanging with him, I feel like I'm with a normal guy. It just goes to show you that it is all about how you look at things."

"I'm glad you are starting to see that."

"Sometimes we need to see things on the outside looking in to truly understand."

The waiter brought us our cokes and I sipped on mine thinking about how things were about to change.

CHAPTER NINETEEN

Don't open locked doors

My phone was ringing and I wondered who would be calling me this early.

"Hell-o?"

"Jude it's me Brice, I heard about what happened with Joey I'm sorry. Listen, I have to ask you a favor, I'm going out of town for a few days and you are the only one I would trust with the house, will you watch it?"

It would be nice to get out of the house for a while, what's the worst thing that could happen? It's right down the street so Mom can't get that worried.

"Alright Brice I'll do it."

I was happy that Brice wasn't treating me like I couldn't do anything, it felt good to be needed.

"Okay, I'm leaving at one so you can bring your stuff here around that time. I don't have many rules just don't drink my beer or go in my study."

"Oh Sir, have you never met me? I'd bring my own beer . . . ."

Brice laughed and the line went dead. I looked at the clock, it was twelve. I had a lot of time to kill so I played Xbox. Luckily, that was one thing I still could do the same way.

I had my dad drop me off at Brice's house at one. It still felt weird to not call it Val's house even in my head I catch myself calling it hers. Brice was just leaving and he wasn't in a tie or anything like that which I found odd. When I was little Dad always wore a dress shirt and pants to work everyday let alone a meeting. I tried not to question his honesty because there had to be a good reason, Brice wouldn't lie to me. I told him to have a good trip and that his house would be the same way he left it when he got back. I closed my eyes for a quick power nap as soon as I heard the door shut. I don't really know when my 'quick nap' turned into full on sleep mode but I think it must have been when I started to dream . . .

"Where can I find the bathroom?"

Val pointed down a hall I hadn't seen yet.

"Down the hall and to your left."

I went down the hall and made a wrong turn. I opened the door without thinking.

It was room with a desk in the middle stacked with papers. I stepped quickly inside the room, shutting the door behind me. I had minutes before Val found me I didn't think I should be in here.

"Jude? What are you doing in here?"

"I was umm, trying to find the bathroom."

"This room is off limits, never come in here again." she said.

It had always hit me weird that Val reacted that way and as I woke up, just like any other person, the first thing I wanted to do was go to the study.

I rolled down the hallway and tried to shake the creepy feeling of being in Val's house. If ever a ghost was going to haunt me, it would so be her. I rolled up to the large door and opened it slowly. It was like I was about to get in trouble and then swung it wide open and rolled in, looking around.

The first thing I spotted was the large desk and all of the papers on it. I really never took Brice as someone who would be so disorganized . . . but his desk was, almost as if he had shuffled through everything in a hurry and left it. I rolled behind it and looked at the first stack and it looked like business stuff and then I spotted a file and reached up and pulled it out. I placed it on my lap and looked down to see Val's name, on a white sticker on the outside of it and took a breath. I had no idea if this was the police record from her suicide or what.

I mustered up the courage to open it and it was something I never expected to see. There was Val, at 8 . . . the photo was black and white, but Val was one of those people that looked the same from childhood on and I stared at her face, so much younger, but still her and then my eyes wandered to the top of it and it read . . .

"Subject 15674."

I narrowed my eyes and looked at her again and flipped the picture to reveal the next page.

"Valerie Vandecamp, age 8 . . . subject seems to show signs of improvement after being brought to the facility, upon receiving her she was very much out of control and violent, with delusions of her parents wanting to kill her. After a few trials with medication, subject seems to be settling into a nice pattern void of outbursts."

"What the hell?" I whispered.

I read on . . .

"Valerie . . . week 10. Subject seems to be quite calm but still suffers from occasional hallucinations of which we are still trying to control with a different mixture of meds and therapy. Valerie seems to think that she is in control of everything around her and is very good at manipulating others into thinking that she is fine, but with constant supervision and monitoring of her sleep patterns, we have decided that another few weeks is recommended to insure a healthy release into society."

I turned the page and another picture of Valerie stared at me . . . only this time she looked older, in fact almost the age she was when I met her.

I looked at the top of the picture again . . .

"Subject 15674"

"Subject . . . Valerie Vandecamp, age 16."

I took a breath and did not know if I wanted to read on or not.

I stared at the page and decided I had too . . .

"Subject seems to be border line schizophrenic with suicidal tendencies, subject admitted by her guardian . . . ie; parent, after she tried to cut him with a knife, believing that he had tried to sexually assault her. Criminal investigation proved this not to be true and the subject has been committed for an indefinite period of time upon which she will be monitored and administered a new medication to try to resolve her paranoia and hallucinations. Father has expressly asked that it be up to the doctors discretion as to when she will be released."

I sat there feeling numb and the anger started to well up in me. The anger towards her Dad, for not telling me . . . then I moved and another picture dropped out. I looked down and shook my head as I stared at it in disbelief.

I held the photo in my hand and started to cry. Valerie sat there with a baby on her lap . . . that of a little girl and I had to wipe my eyes to even understand what I was looking at, although I had probably already guessed.

"Subject 15674"

"Valerie Vandecamp. Subject gave birth at the facility and without clearance from the doctors, child has been taken to live with a suitable foster family. Valerie has yet to reveal the Father and for some time claimed it to be a child she had with her own Dad. Genetic testing proved this to be not true and without her guardian stepping in, the child was removed from her. Guardian was notified but refused to visit the child after birth and wants nothing to do with the situation. Valerie has shown great improvement and is up for a board hearing in 3 weeks."

I dropped the file and started to roll out, slamming into the door and almost knocking myself onto the floor. I rolled down the hallway and stopped, still catching my breath and then I pulled out my phone, completely out of breath and called my Dad.

"Jude? You okay."

"Come and get me . . . . please Dad, get me now." I said and with that he hung up and I dropped the phone to the floor and started to cry harder than I ever thought that I could.

CHAPTER TWENTY

Scared to relive

I sat in the office and my dad kept glancing at me and I had nothing to say . . . nothing at all. In fact, I had not talked to anyone for two weeks and I had barely ate and now I was here . . . in a shrinks office, waiting to have some jackass ask me all the questions I had no intention of answering for anyone. Then the door opened and a woman stepped out, nice legs as I could see and I looked at them and then she smiled at me and looked at my dad.

"If you don't mind, perhaps Jude and I could speak alone." she said to my Dad and he nodded and stood up as I pushed myself, refusing to accept any help at all.

I followed the hottie down the hallway and then to a room to the right and she opened the door and I rolled past her into a beautiful room, all decked out in art and greenery . . . very soothing and with good purpose. I stopped and looked back at her.

"I really don't want to be here."

"Oh I know." she said as she walked to her desk and sat down. I sat there waiting for whatever was going to come next.

She opened a file and looked at it and I laughed.

"What is so funny?" she asked all nice and calm.

"File . . . it's on me, right?"

"Well . . . it is actually. I sat down with your parents before today and we discussed things."

"Like Jude things." I muttered.

"Like things that would and could help you Jude." she said.

I laughed again and rolled up to her desk and sat there staring at her.

"I am not crazy, I am just tired of shit."

"You want to define shit?" she asked me and I smiled to hear her cuss.

"Well, you probably have it all there." I said as I looked at her file.

"What I have here is facts, not you Jude. You are not purely a fact, you are human being with feelings . . ."

I interrupted her.

"I don't feel anything, I don't want to." I said.

She leaned up and looked at me.

"Feelings are like water, they ebb and flow whether we want them to or not."

"Deep . . . can I go now?"

She smiled and leaned back in her chair.

"Believe it or not I am here to help you."

"You are getting paid."

She tapped her pen on the desk.

"That is fact, I do get paid to help those who need it, and Jude . . . you are one of those people, whether you want to say it or not."

"Well you are good." I said as I laughed at her.

"Do you want to tell me about why you find it hard to commit?" she said out of the blue.

"Oh hell no." I said as I started to roll towards the door, she stood up slowly and then stepped in front of me and blocked my way.

"Ummm . . . move." I said to her.

"You cannot commit, in fact I would guess that sex is just something you have, isn't it?" she said to me.

"I feel like that is none of your damn business."

"How about the fact that you feel like it is your fault that Valerie is dead." she said and that stopped my heart in my chest. I looked at her with such anger.

"I suggest that you shut the fuck up and get out of my way." I said and she moved for me and I jerked the door open and rolled out.

CHAPTER TWENTY ONE

Free

The next few days were hell. I still wasn't eating or sleeping. Flashes of Val's file crept in my mind as soon as I closed my eyes. The phone rang off the hook it was mainly Brice. He left me a voicemail asking why I didn't watch his house. The guy was a bastard and could die tomorrow for all I care. It'd be no skin off my ass. I don't owe him anything and he owes me everything, nothing he could say would change that. I got on the floor of my room and leaned on my door, holding my head in my hands I felt a cry coming and once I started, I knew it would be hard to stop. There was a knock at my door and I stayed where I was, blocking entry into my room.

"Jude, someone is here to see you . . . ."

"Tell Brice to fuck off."

"Jude, it's me."

"Go away Wendy, I don't want you here."

"Jude, I'm here because I care about you."

I closed my eyes and let my mind take me to a simpler time . . . .

"Val, the past few weeks have been amazing and I'm starting to really feel something for you."

Val leaned her head on my chest and sighed with a bright smile.

"I've been waiting for you to realize you care about me for a long time, it feels great to finally hear it."

I sat up and leaned in to speak.

"I care about you more than you will ever know, Miss. Vandecamp . . . ."

Val kissed me hard on the mouth till I was dizzy.

"Jude, let me in . . . ."

I knew she was talking about more ways than one.

"No."

"I never told you, I'm a black belt."

If I was in a normal state of mind then I would find that a very big turn on but not today.

"You wouldn't."

"Try me."

I sighed and scooted away from the door, knowing she wouldn't leave till I did. Wendy walked in and tried to help me back into my chair but I wouldn't let her so she sat across from me in the middle of my floor.

"I guess you've been keeping tabs on me like a creep, huh?"

"I didn't ask anyone to give me that information, Jude . . . ."

"Oh great, so my parents willingly told you, that makes it so much better."

"They only told me that you found out something about Valerie and it broke you."

"You can't break what's already broken . . . ."

"Jude, talk to me . . . . it's okay."

Wendy reached for my hand and I pulled away from her.

"Don't."

"Let me help . . . ."

"She was fucking crazy Wendy."

'What do you mean?"

"Brice had a file, it was all about her."

"Oh Jude, come here, if you don't want to talk about it I understand."

Wendy embraced me as I literally cried on her shoulder.

"EVERYTHING WAS A LIE . . . . everything. I bet she didn't even love me."

"Jude don't talk like that . . . ."

"And why the hell not?"

I moved back a couple inches to look at her with a blank stare.

"Because you are hurt and upset, you don't mean what you say."

"Wendy get your head out of your ass, this is real shit quit acting like a shrink."

Wendy put her hand on my shoulder like you see doctors do on TV. I took a deep breath and started to regain control.

"Did you know?"

"W-what?"

"About her."

"What are you talking about?"

"They both knew, and didn't even tell me." I muttered.

"Knew what Jude?"

I thought about Brice once again knowing he was just as guilty as Val for not stepping in and stopping the unhealthy relationship. I should have known the truth from day one. I would never get the years back they stole from me and that, that was what made me angry the most.

"I LOVED HER, AND-AND SHE JUST WALKED ALL OVER ME!!!!!"

"I know you miss her." Wendy said.

I looked at her and shook my head.

"Miss her? She was a crazy bitch and her Dad is just as crazy."

"What is it Jude?" Wendy said.

"Wendy . . . ." I took a deep breath. "Val was committed to an asylum."

"Well, a lot of people are Jude."

"You don't get it. She lived there over and over again."

"I knew she had been committed Jude."

I looked at Wendy and could feel the pain in my chest again.

"There was a baby."

Wendy stared at me. "I know Jude, your baby."

"Oh my god Wendy! Not that one . . . there was a child before mine!"

"What?" Wendy said as she leaned forward.

"She had it in the asylum and Brice didn't step in to do anything about it . . . . they gave it away Wendy!" I yelled as the tears continued.

"Oh my god." Wendy muttered as she stared at me and reached out to touch me. I moved and wiped my eyes.

Wendy sat still letting me get it all out.

"Don't you get it, Jude? She walked over all of us and she made all of us love her. You've said it yourself."

Wendy was trying to make me feel better and we both knew it would never work.

"It's one thing to say something but to see it with your own eyes is a different story."

"Jude maybe you needed to see it with your own eyes to truly see it for what it is, a bad thing that happened to a very good person."

"I will never understand why they did this to me, just as I will never understand why you care about me."

Wendy's eyes turned glossy as she was about to cry.

"I wish I knew. We all do. The only way to get the answers is to ask Brice."

"I can't, I won't."

Wendy cupped my face in her hands and fought back tears once more.

"You will wake up everyday and wonder what you did to deserve it, I can't let you live like that. It nearly killed me."

"Wendy I-I don't know what to say I would deck the dick square in the mouth if I ever ran into him."

"That is not the point, Jude. The point is, you need to talk to Brice."

"Swear to me Jude."

I moved closer and let my lips touch hers with caution.

"I swear."

Chapter Twenty Two

Drunken confessions

"At least you will die knowing her for what she was, a manipulative little bitch."

It was dark and his hands were pounding my face in. My nose made a loud crack and blood spattered everywhere. The man gave a wicked laugh as he stabbed me in the heart, there was a horrible scream and I fell to the ground, dying on the cold bloody floor.

I woke up and felt myself shaking and my voice was hoarse.

"Holy shit, he killed me."

I got out of bed pulled a shirt on that was left on my floor from a week ago. I rolled to the bathroom and splashed water on my face, hoping to forget the dream that was now burned in my memory. I bent down and got my toothbrush and toothpaste from under the sink. Just as I was about to sit back up and put toothpaste on my toothbrush I saw something that I was about a hundred percent sure I had thrown out when Val died. I turned on the light just to make sure what I saw was really there and not just my eyes playing tricks on me, nope still there. I picked up Val's secret toothbrush and let the memory flood in . . .

"Okay, okay, okay. As much as I would love to spend the whole day with you, I have to get dressed now. Dad is coming home. He's on leave for the week so I have to look nice."

I got out of bed and slipped my boxers back on.

"I don't see anything wrong with what you are wearing."

Val smiled as she looked at her favorite pair of boxers she brought me for my birthday, one year.

I turned my back to her.

"I do look pretty sexy don't I? But I don't think that would make you number one on my Dad's list."

"Hum, this is a shame because I have the perfect bra and underwear to match you."

I laughed and started to walk to the bathroom grabbing my toothbrush and hitting 'on'.

"Hey baby, I was thinking maybe I could bring some of my stuff here, you know if we want to make this more official . . . ."

I stepped out of the bathroom with my toothbrush still on and in my mouth. I gave her a nod and she smiled wrapping a sheet around her and getting out of bed to pick up her crop-top and jeans.

"Okay well I'm going to head out the way I came, I'll call you and if you're lucky I may be free again tonight."

I crossed my fingers hoping she was.

I turned on my toothbrush and with the other hand I messed with my hair, finally giving up since I was still sweaty from the nightmare. I headed to the kitchen where the phone was ringing off the hook, wonder who that is . . . .

"Hello?"

"Jude, I can't believe you actually picked up. I've been calling you for days, I saw you didn't stay at the house . . . . if it was too much for you, I'm sorry I asked. It's hard for me to be there sometimes because I miss her so bad."

"Wait . . . I'm sorry but you have got to be fucking kidding me . . ."

"Excuse me?"

"You heard me, how dare you say you miss her."

"Jude, I know it's been hard but you aren't the only one that loved her."

"Oh Brice believe me I know the whole damn town loved her or should I say nailed her."

"Watch your tone with me, boy. She was my daughter. I am the one that found her laying on the bathroom floor."

"Like I care anymore." I muttered to him.

"What?" Brice said continuing to get angry.

"You heard me Brice . . . I don't care."

There was a moment of silence and then the phone went dead and I stared at it and then hoped like hell he wasn't on his way over.

I rolled to the window and I'll be damned if he didn't come driving up in his car. He got out with it still on and it tried to roll away on him and he scrambled back into the drivers seat and stopped it. He then left his door open and came walking with a disgusted look on his face towards my door.

"Oh shit." I said as I rolled towards the door and he started to pound on it. I have no idea why bravery kicked in, but it did and I opened it up and stared him down.

Brice took a breath and then tried to speak calmly although I could see his chest rising and falling.

"Would you like to explain your attitude to me son?"

"I am not your son and this is my house Brice."

Brice narrowed his eyes.

"If your were standing I would hit you in the mouth."

I laughed.

"Big man." I said to him.

"Don't push me." Brice muttered.

"Seriously?" I said to him as I shook my head.

"You need to leave and not come back here ever!" I yelled at him.

"You owe me an explanation and an apology!" Brice yelled.

"OH! Fuck you!" I yelled at him.

He lunged at me and knocked me from the chair and we rolled on the floor. I hit him in the face and he tried to block me but my knuckles connected with his mouth and it instantly started to bleed. He then rolled behind me and grabbed my arms, holding me still and I screamed.

"Jude . . . calm down!" he yelled at me.

"Me? You jumped me you fucking psychotic!"

"What?"

"Psychotic! Just like Valerie."

Brice released me and stood up, looking down on me.

"You went into my study didn't you?" he asked me.

"Damn straight I did." I said as I pushed myself up.

"I asked you to not do that."

I looked up at him and grimaced.

"Asked me? Like you the right to ask me anything Brice. As far as I am concerned, you are the reason Val is dead."

With that Brice stumbled back from me and left my house. I watched him go and before he drove away I slammed my door.

I sat in my house for quite sometime and then I decided that a drink was due . . . hell it was more than due, it had been earned. I cleaned myself up and out I went, ready for a night of old Jude, the one who could pound the beers and pass out.

I rolled up to the bar and looked at it knowing this was not the best idea when you are upset, but for me a good night of not remembering would maybe help in some twisted way. I pushed the door open and heard the familiar music and laughter and rolled up to a table and waited, hoping Drake would spot me and he did. He came over quickly with my favorite beer in hand and a pitcher and placed them in front of me. I looked up at him and he pulled up a chair and turned it like he usually does and smiled at me.

"You look like shit." he said as he laughed.

"I have been better." I said as I took a huge drink of the beer and before I knew it I had chugged it gone.

"Damn man." Drake said as he filled my glass again.

"Lets hear it." he said as he leaned forward and stared at me.

"You ever been to point of not giving a shit about anything?" I asked him.

Drake laughed.

"Most days." he said as he stood up and grabbed himself a glass and decided to join me.

He filled his glass and then took a huge swig of it and then slammed it down on the table.

"Tell me . . . is it that little hottie you have been hanging out with?" he asked me.

"Wendy? No." I said as I pounded another beer and slammed the glass down on the table.

"What is it then?" Drake asked.

"Fucking Valerie man." I muttered.

"Oh hell Jude, seriously? You need to let that go man." he said.

I stared at him and shook my head.

"I wish that I could . . . you know I loved her."

"I know man, you said it a thousand times." Drake said as he re-filled both of our glasses and cleared his throat.

He raised his glass to me.

"A toast to a nice piece of tail." he said and he clicked his glass against mine and I stared him down. He chugged and then looked at me as he wiped his mouth.

"What?" he asked me.

"I don't know why you said it like that." I said to him.

Drake looked at me all glossy eyed from drinking to much.

"You said she was great in the sack."

"No . . . in fact I never talked to you about sex with her, she was the only one."

"Oh hell Jude!" Drake said as he stood up and walked back over to the bar getting us another pitcher of beer. I watched him and played with the glass on my table. Drake returned and sat down, re-filling both glasses and then he took a drink and eyed me. I sat there staring at him.

"Dude, seriously . . . what the hell?" I asked him.

Drank chugged his beer and slammed it down on the table.

"Jude . . . man." he said quietly as he shook his head.

I leaned up and continued to stare at him.

"Is there something we need to talk about?" I asked him.

Drake sighed and leaned back.

"I banged her man." Drake said, and I almost couldn't understand him.

"Excuse me?" I said to him.

Drake leaned up.

"I banged her Jude, before you . . . . and after."

"What the fuck?!" I yelled at him.

"Jude . . . Valerie was a crazy bitch, you had to know."

"No . . . no, NO Drake, I did not know about you."

Drake stood up and held out his hand to me. I hit it away from me.

"Jude . . . don't be all shitty."

I laughed, probably harder than I had laughed in a long time . . . I started to roll away and then I stopped.

"Get me a case to go . . . you owe me you dick." I said.

Drake went to the bar and came back with a case and set it on my lap.

"I wanted to tell you, before now." he said.

I shook my head and rolled away from him, ready to find a nice secluded spot to drink myself to death.

CHAPTER TWENTY THREE

Brothers that jail together, stay together

I was sitting in Sunset Beach State Park at around midnight.

It was the little things Val did, like watching Avatar over and over again without a word. Bringing me coffee to class with cute little notes on the cup.

I lifted the tab on the Miller Light, pop, sizzle, slam, gone.

Her lips, her eyes, the way she tossed her hair in the wind. Pop, sizzle, slam . . . . Buying me the Xbox for Christmas when my parents wouldn't. Then staying up with me playing Call of Duty till three in the morning. Pop, sizzle, slam, gone. Her kisses were so sweet and satisfying I could have kissed her everyday for the rest of my life but because of Brice I would never kiss her again. Pop, sizzle, slam, gone. I felt like I was on top of the world when I was with her, nothing could touch me. Which is why it is ironic, everything can touch me now. Pop, sizzle, slam, gone.

The beer went though my blood steam and I started to feel numb inside and out. I picked up the empty beer cans and tossed them at a tree. Brice is a killer and should not be allowed to live. Clink, smash, gone. I grabbed the next beer can. Joey took my life and turned it upside down. He took the only good things about it and threw them away like trash. He is the worse brother in the world. Clink, smash, gone. Val only cared about herself, she never once thought about me. Clink, smash, gone. My dad left me to be the man of the house when I couldn't even take take of myself. Clink, smash, gone.

"I love you, Jude."

I stared at her naked body thinking about how perfect it was, like a work of art. It wasn't fair to the rest of the world that I was the one enjoying it. I kissed her just below her boob.

"If I spend the rest of my life in a box on the side of the road, at least I'll wake up to your pretty face, love."

"Jude, that's sweet but Valerie Lee Vandecamp doesn't live in anything but the best."

"Then you shall have anything your heart desires."

"I want you to take me, now, Jude."

I pulled at the sleeve of my shirt as I watched the beer fall from my lap. Not remembering why I had beer in my bed when I was about to make love to an amazing woman I think that trumps beer any day. I lifted my shirt over my head and smiled at Val who was feet away from me now. I unzipped my jeans and pulled them off, I was going to do the same to my boxers but then I saw something very odd. I was in a wheelchair, not my bed.

"Hey, baby, I didn't know tonight was doctor. I think I like the fireman theme better, I mean you look smokin' in yellow and a doctor's coat is hard to rip off. On second thought, as long as I'm in this chair I bet your cute little ass could give one hell of a lap dance."

I patted my lap and started to move towards where I saw Val disappear.

"Oh Valerie, I'm ready . . . . come out, come out where ever you are."

I started to roll into town hoping I would find her, she liked to do this often it was her own little game of foreplay, it drove me crazy.

"Val, I'm almost in pain over here waiting for you, a man has needs you know . . . ."

I looked around and saw an older version of Val on the sidewalk, I rolled up to her.

"I'm so happy I found you, now we can get it on."

"Honey, I don't think I'm the one you're looking for but I can show you just as good of a time for a price."

"I told you I don't like the doctor then again, we've never played hooker, I may like it."

"Listen kid, I can be whoever you want if you throw the cash but if not get lost."

"Ha-ha very funny Val, now cut the shit and have sex with me."

She rolled her eyes and walked away from me. I called after her for a long time and finally gave up, I slid out of my chair and passed out on the street, knowing she would find me sooner or later.

*   *   *

I woke up to laughing, not really sure where I was.

"Holy shit the cripple is wasted off his ass . . . ."

"Well Buzz, wouldn't you be if you were in this ugly chair your whole life?"

"Yeah, no shit, Stan. If only I had the money to get smashed . . . ."

"Now you do, isn't this what we came for?"

The one called Stan picked up my wallet and started going though it. I guess the inner Chuck Norris came out because I punched Stan right in the face.

"Damn, for a cripple, he's got game . . . ."

"Oh shut up, Buzz. Lets knock him out and split."

Buzz walked closer to me and stepped on my face, breaking my nose. I put my right hand to my face and used my left to hit him in the balls. Buzz fell to the ground, holding himself. Stan, who recovered from his hit, tried to swing at me, knocking me out. The last thing I heard were sirens.

*   *   *

This time I woke up in a jail cell, I banged my hands on the bars.

"Hey you, why the hell am I here?"

"For public intoxication, you were a .22, way over the limit."

I didn't really remember much but being jumped, it didn't help that I was still drunk.

I started checking out the cell hoping my cellmate wasn't some scary dude that could kick my ass if I looked at him the wrong way. I saw a guy at the far end of the cell, no, it couldn't be . . . . oh fuck, it is.

"Joseph?"

My brother's head snapped up at the sound of my voice.

"Oh Jude, brother, you don't know how much I've missed you."

His words made me sick, anger built up inside me but I didn't wear it on my face, no, I had a better idea.

"Come here and give me hug, I'm so glad to see you're okay."

Joey walked over and bumped his body to mine, that was as close to a hug we could get because of the handcuffs. I lifted my hands and smacked him in the jaw.

"We are far from even, brother."

I smiled as he cussed under his breath.

"You have no idea how much joy this brings me to be with you in this cell. It will be a long night, dick."

"You are sick, Jude."

"Karma is a bitch."

I hit him again even harder than before in the eye. It turned blue right away. I laughed, knowing he wouldn't fight back and I could go on forever. It felt good to get out all the hate I had been holding inside.

Joey started to sob as the blood flowed harder, so did his tears.

"Brother, brother . . . . .please . . . . . . I beg you . . . . if you are going to kill me . . . . .do it fast."

I stared down at my bloody hands, I knew I had a temper but I didn't know I was capable of something so monsterous.

"I can't kill you, dumb ass, I'm not looking to spend the rest of my life in jail."

His head was swaying back and forth like a punching bag.

"Why did you do this?" I asked him, the punches slowing down as I spoke.

"I-I don't kn-ow."

"Wrong answer . . . ."

I kind of felt bad as I delivered the final punch that knocked him out. How does that make me any better than him? I am impaired today and he was impaired on that day.

Joey opened his eyes and starred at me then to my dismay, he smiled, his teeth full of blood.

"Listen dude, I've had a lot of time to think in here and I really am sorry for what I did, Jude I was fucked up."

"Come here, bro . . ."

Joey stood up with a laugh.

"As long as you don't hit me."

Joey came over and bumped his body to mine again.

"This is a new start, Joey; I want us to be brothers."

"You know it, bro."

There was a tap on the bars.

"Jude Franklin, someone paid your bail."

I rolled out of the cell and saw Wendy waiting for me.

"Oh Wendy . . . . ."

I wanted to kiss her but I remembered my breath smelled like I lived in a beer can for ten years.

"I'm glad to see you're okay."

"Yeah well, almost okay."

I pointed to my nose with a laugh.

"I think it makes you look manly."

We got in the car and headed to the beach, we did not dare sit at the bar. Wendy pulled a bottle of water and gum out of her bag with a warm smile.

"Thanks . . ."

"Jude, its okay I don't think badly of you."

"Shh, Wendy, I don't want to talk about it."

I put my hand to my forehead, blocking the sun from my eyes.

"I think you should lay down."

We laid in the sand and for once I felt safe.

Chapter twenty Four

Object of anger

I rolled into the house around midnight and the living room light turned on. It was my Dad waiting up for me.

"Jude, I got a call from the cops last night at three in the morning about you being drunk, you're lucky I didn't tell your Mother, her heart can't take it. We are going for a drive, son."

We got in the car and Dad sighed, starting in on me.

"Jude, one day you will be a father and husband, you need to learn to deal with things without alcohol."

"How do you?"

"I try to think of every time I over drink as one less day of my life."

"Damn, that's dark."

"Yes it is, I hope you think of that next time . . . ."

"I can't believe you see it like that when you see a friend die every day."

"I'd hate to beat all the odds of war then die because of something I could control. Why did you drink last night?"

"I don't know Dad."

"Yes you do . . ." he said.

"No I don't."

"This game doesn't work on me, now spit it out."

Dad stopped in a parking lot and looked me deep in the eyes.

"My friend Drake told me he slept with Val and it was too much to handle."

"Someone tipped the cops off and I think I know who."

"No, Dad, Drake has been my friend for years. He would never do that to me."

Plus, he gave me the beer.

"Well, who told the cops is not what's worrying me, I'm just glad they did. Let me tell you if I ever hear of you getting picked up drunk again, your ass is grass, you hear me?"

I knew my Dad wasn't telling me not to drink, he was telling me to be smart about it. That's what I like most about him, he knows what I do because he did it too. He's not one of the 'do as I say not as I do' types of parents. Everyone knows that never works.

"Yes Sir."

"Now with that being said, I'm leaving again soon and I'm worried about your Mom."

"Dad, I will take care of her."

"No, you've been the rock for too long . . . ."

He was right but if Mom needed someone, I would be there above everything else.

"I don't understand."

"Jude, I love your Mother more than anything in this world but you are my son and I haven't been a dad to you or Joey, part of this is my fault. That is why I'm telling your Mom to go live with Aunt Paula in New Jersey."

For the first time in my life, I saw my Dad cry and I knew as much as it would hurt to send Mom away, it had to be done.

"You're right."

My dad looked like he had just been shot in the heart, I could tell he was about to break down. I embraced him. My dad could be the best in the whole Army but this was what I will always respect him the most for.

"I love you, Dad."

"I am so proud of you son, you are the man I always hoped you would be."

My Dad may have missed half of my childhood but the least I could do was try to let him make up for lost times.

*   *   *

I rolled into Brix Wines like I owned the place. To pissed off to care that people were starring at me, I was used to it. I tapped on the bar and Drake went to get me a beer before I stopped him.

"I won't be needing that today, actually I was hoping to have a word with you . . . ."

"Shit, you would think a night in jail makes a guy tougher not softer."

Drake was trying to act like everything was fine but little did he know, I knew the truth and I wasn't backing down till I heard him say every word. I turned around and out the door, Drake followed me.

"Alright, asshole, I know what you did, now spill . . . ."

I pulled Drake up to the wall and looked him straight in the eyes. He smiled and started to laugh.

"Come on Jude, you've known me for four years, if you really think you can fight me, well your just plain crazy."

I knew I could fight Drake if that's what it came down to, in the past two day I have beat the shit out of Joey and Brice. Drake may be tall and lean but as far as muscles go he could spend a year in a gym and it wouldn't help. Basically, he's all talk and no game.

"Tell me the truth, why did you call the cops on me when you gave me the beer?"

"It was a warning, you would have gotten picked up anyway but I wanted to make sure you didn't drop my name. See, it hurts business and I can't have unhappy druggies, you know what that's like. They can go somewhere else but I won't make money like that anywhere."

"Damn, I knew you were low but really Drake?"

"Listen, I'm apart of a underground club on Drew Street called The Hole. We mostly drink and gamble, they are people just like you and me, Jude, they love to party. I think you would be perfect and a member just died so you're in luck, are you with me?"

I punched him, this new found macho stuff is really working out nicely.

"I'll never join you."

Well growing up, I always wanted to be Luke Skywalker so the line sort of just came out. I let go of Drake's shirt, he let himself fall to the ground and I rolled to the beach. I grabbed my phone and gripped it with anger, my knuckles turned white. I hit the number of the one person I knew could help me compress my feelings for a few hours anyway.

"Hey, it's me, I was thinking we could get out of here for awhile . . . ."

"Are you sure you're okay Jude?"

"Yeah totally, I just want some time with you is all . . . ."

"No, you want to see how fast we can steam up the car windows and this is the part where I should tell you that there is more to us than sex but today I happen to feel the same way."

"Pick me up at Sunset Beach."

I hit 'end' and rubbed my hands together, trying to get the sweat off.

It was about a half hour before Wendy pulled up in a BMW which looked brand new. I smiled, this was one sports car I had not slept with anyone in.

"Nice car."

"Yeah, Dad flew it in from London, it was his from high school and he couldn't get rid of it."

"Wow, lucky us, huh?"

"I'll say . . . ."

It took us six hours but we ended up at Mammoth Mountain we made small talk the whole way there. Wendy looked out the window and she couldn't believe her eyes.

"Jude, it's snowing!!"

We got out of the car and Wendy started throwing snowballs at me.

"Wendy, this is not fair, I don't have a coat."

Wendy put her snowball down and I bent down, got snow and threw it at her.

"Got yah . . ."

"Jude Franklin, you will pay . . . ."

"I hope so, angry sex is the best kind, why do you think I called you?"

Wendy put her hands on her hips and stood inches from my face.

"What is troubling you, Jude? Why did you lie to me?"

I held my hands up to my face.

"My friend at the bar, Drake. Val cheated on me with him and he never told me."

"Then why are we here about to have sex when you are so upset?"

"Because, this is what I do Wendy, run away from things with sex and beer. Besides, why does this matter to you? You were the one that talked of steaming up windows and shit."

"That was before, I will not be the object of your anger."

"Okay fine, I'm upset but you always know how to get my mind off things so . . . ."

I rolled a inch closer to her and put my arms out, she slapped them away.

"So nothing, as much as I would love to have sex with you right now, I can't."

I put on my charm face and tried again.

"But Wendy, look at the view, the snow and that sexy car, it all screams 'jump me'."

"Not going to work Jude."

I gave the bottom lip at a last ditch attempted.

"Really Jude, how old are you?"

Wendy smiled and sat in my lap, I put my arms around her, knowing that I didn't win but she was here and with the day that I was having, that's all that mattered. I kissed her on the head, she turned to look at me.

"See how nice it is when you play along?"

"I'll be the first to say, I'm actually warming up to it."

Wendy put her hand on my cheek, there was something about her touch, it was not forceful or seductive, it was pure. I felt like I could be here forever. Out here there was no drama or broken legs, it was just Jude and Wendy.

"Don't let me push you away, no matter what."

"No matter what." Wendy said.

The snow started to fall harder than before from the taller mountains above us and feeling that the moment was right, I kissed Wendy softly on the mouth. She took the bull by the horns and the kiss deepened. If this was a movie normally the parents would cover the eyes of little children as we stripped by now but I actually wanted to keep it PG it felt nice for a change. I think the reason I hide behind sex is that maybe I am scared to feel something other than horny. That is going to stop today.

"I changed my mind, throw me in the back seat, Jude."

"No, you were right, angry sex is okay for whores but you are a lady Wendy, and I want to treat you like one."

"Forget that middle aged shit, you were right this mountain screams 'jump me'."

"No."

All this fighting sort of turned me on but I had to compose myself, I knew what was the right thing to do, now if only I have the control to do it, or not do it I should say.

"We should go home, I bet our parents are wondering where we are."

"But I want to stay, can't we stay Jude?"

"I wish, but not today."

Wendy got up from my lap and guided me to the car, making sure I didn't fall. We got in the car and turned on the radio, *Sexy and I Know It* came on which didn't help the no angry sex thing.

CHAPTER TWENTY FIVE

From all directions

I was in my room, in fact, I was in the same spot I had been in for almost two days now, thinking about Drake and that damn club. Part of me wanted to see if it was real or some made up bull shit to get kids in gangs. The old me would not have given a rat's ass if Drake treated me like shit or not. It was because it was a place to party, but ever since I spent the night in jail beating my brother's head in, I really haven't wanted a drink. Still, I could use a night on the town and maybe I would meet some new people, if Drake showed up I'd leave.

Then my phone rang and looked down at it to see the number I never wanted to see . . . Brice. I had to laugh out loud, wondering why the hell he felt like it was okay to even think about contacting me. I started to hit the "ignore" button and accidently hit the answer and I heard his voice as I looked at the phone in my hand.

"JUDE!" he yelled out and I narrowed my eyes and stared at it.

"JUDE PLEASE!" he yelled again and I looked at the phone and then it put it up to my ear feeling like a complete fool.

"What?" I said with a malicious tone.

"Jude . . . oh my god, please I need your help . . . please."

"You are kidding me right?" I said.

"NO . . . listen I know you hate me and you probably should, but I am in trouble . . . please Jude."

"You are in trouble?" I said, sounding like I half did not care and half did not believe him.

"Jude . . . listen, please . . . I need money . . . I need money now, or they are . . ."

His voice trailed off and an unfamiliar voice got on the line with a slight eastern accent.

"Jude . . . your friend has made a very bad mistake."

I rolled my eyes and sighed.

"Brice is a dick." I said.

"Oh really?" the anonymous man said and I heard Brice scream in the background as a loud crack rang out. Then I heard Brice call out Val's name and I knew he was hurt for real.

"Wait! . . . wait." I said.

The man laughed on the phone and I waited.

"Well, Jude . . . we will do this, since Brice called you and it was the only call that was offered to him I am assuming you are close and I will tell you his arm is now shattered."

"What?" I said out of disbelief.

"Yes, he fell down."

"He did not fall down." I said getting irritated.

"Well . . . accidents do happen." he said.

I sat there and then the anger that I felt for Brice started to well back up in me.

"You know what? Break everything on him, the bastard deserves it." I said.

The man hesitated and then I heard a voice I should not be hearing at all. It was Wendy calling out to me.

"Wait! Wendy?" I yelled into the phone.

"Oh . . . is that someone you care about?" the man said.

"Listen I don't know what the fuck is going on, but you touch her or hurt her in any way . . ."

He interrupted me. "Oh, she is so pretty Jude and you would be surprised what a man will tell you when he is in pain . . . . Brice has told us many things about you and this beautiful girl of yours."

"God damn it! Put her on the phone!" I yelled out to him.

"Jude . . . I need for you to come down to 3475 Jefferson street, by the waterfront. Tell no one, no cops and bring 2,000 with you."

I laughed. "2,000 as in dollars? I don't have that!"

"Oh okay." he said to me and I heard Wendy scream out.

"Wait! . . . wait!" I yelled. I could hear Wendy start to sob in the background and the man waited for me.

"Brice said you would know where to find the money and I would suggest that you do, or he and your girlfriend will die . . . be here in 2 hours or attend their funerals." he said and he hung up as I yelled out to Wendy in the phone.

I sat there stunned and my mind was racing. What the hell is going on? Why the hell is Brice calling me and how dare he give them Wendy . . . how dare him. I felt a panic attack coming on and then it hit me. In Brice's study there was a wall safe . . . . he must have money in it, he has too.

I rolled up to the house and foolishly I turned the knob, nope locked. I picked up a rock and threw it at the window closest to the door. I stuck my hand in the broken window and unlocked the door. I heard the sound that I was so used to when the door opened, so did the memories I was trying so hard to keep out.

*   *   *

"Why can't I just sneak in the window?"

"Because Dad put rose bushes under my window."

"Well I much rather get cut than lose my head after I wake up your Dad. No sex and a call home, doesn't that just scream 'Best Friday ever'?"

"He forgets to lock the door all the time also he's a very hard sleeper."

"With my luck this is the one day he will lock the door or he won't and wake up to his daughter's new boyfriend trying to have sex with her at odd hours of the night. That will really make him love me."

"Jude, you won't be sorry I'm sure I'll be better with the home field advantage."

"Okay I'm sold but Val?"

"Yes?"

"Don't keep me waiting."

I turned the door knob and ran upstairs in a dance like fashion, making sure to be light on my feet. I was glad it was dark and no one could see me because I looked really gay, oh well in about a minute I was going to be all man. I opened the door to what I thought was Val's room but she was never clear about if it was on the right or left.

"Oh Val, I'm ready to . . . ."

I saw a stalky man with grey hair and a five o'clock shadow, I'm guessing this is Val's Dad. I turned to run down the stairs out the door when he sat up.

"Who are you?" he asked me as he looked at his nightstand surely thinking about pulling out his gun.

"Jude Franklin, Sir."

"Alright Jude Franklin, I'm going to give you two seconds to tell we why you are here or I'm calling the cops."

"I was going to see Valerie."

"That's impossible, I told her to stay away from boys, they're no good for her. If you want to keep your head I think you should get the hell out of my house boy."

I ran as fast as I could home making a mental note to tell Val that I don't care how good she thinks she will be in her own bed we are waiting awhile, sex isn't in the cards right now.

Funny isn't it? That first night that I met Brice he hated me at first and now I'm saving his life. I rolled in the house and went straight to the study. I had to block all the papers tossed around the room out of my mind, I was here for one thing and one thing only.

I rolled up to the safe and started trying different patterns on the keypad, getting mad at each failed attempt. I hit the safe a few times. Then I remembered there was one thing I didn't try, Val's birthday. I punched the numbers in hoping this was the right code and just as I did, the door swung open. I couldn't believe someone would keep so much money in a safe. I grabbed a little over $2,000 as I would need a cab ride. As I took the money, I saw a black gun buried under it. I picked it up and turned it over, making sure the magazine was full. I tucked the gun in the waste line of my shorts. Then I called for a cab.

"Yes, I would like a cab sent to 24783 Sunrise Drive."

"We will be there as soon as we can, Sir."

"A extra twenty dollars if you can make it here in three minutes."

I hit 'end' and went outside, it was the longest three minutes of my life. When the cab got there I hurried and told the guy how to fold the chair. I got in the car all by myself, but I didn't have the time to be proud. I gave the guy the address and money along with the twenty I added ten and told him to run every red light. As soon as I saw the waterfront and a very ugly, rundown warehouse I knew I had made it. The guy helped me out on the street with my chair, I told him thank you and he drove away.

CHAPTER TWENTY SIX

Never the same

I saw a guy standing with his back to me and I fought the need to pull out the gun and shoot him on the spot. I slowly rolled up to the man and he turned and smiled the creepiest smile I have ever seen.

"You must be Jude, glad you could join us. Follow me right this way and watch where you are rolling we would hate for you to fall."

Okay you have got to be shitting me, this guy is acting like a zombie, isn't he suppose to be putting a blindfold on me and pushing me into the fire pit by now?

"Your friends are in good hands trust me, you'll see. The ones who come in never want to come out, bless their hearts it nearly kills them to leave."

The guy opened the door and walked in, I followed as I was told.

"Bill, can you show Mr. Franklin where it is his friends are staying?"

Bill was a very tall and musclier man with tattoos up and down his arms. Now this is more what I pictured in my head. He grabbed my arm and pulled me to a dark room lit by candles. He let go of my arm and held out his hand.

"Give me the money."

I reached in my pocket and was about to pull out the money then I heard Wendy.

"Jude, they are going to kill us anyway, don't do it."

Bill walked over to Wendy and hit her in the face. I wanted to attack Bill but I knew that Bill wasn't the one doing this and I wanted to get the guy in charge. I tossed the money on the ground, Bill picked it up and walked away.

"Jude, Brice is hurt, you have to help."

I didn't want to help Brice but I knew if he was loose they would forget about us and go chase him, we could escape. I rolled over to Brice and slid out of my chair to check for a heart beat, not there. Lucky my gym teacher was hot so I always was awake when we did CPR. I pounded on his chest and his heart started beating again.

"Brice, listen to me, I'm going to untie you and I need you to run."

"Jude . . . ." Brice said weakly in my ear.

The knot on the rope was really tight and it took me four times to free Brice's hands. Brice didn't even move and try to get the rope off his feet so I did it for him.

"Brice you're free, now go."

Brice stumbled to his feet and he grabbed at me, steadying himself. He looked at me with such sorrow in his eyes, as if he wanted to say 'I am sorry for everything', but truth was I would not have even come if Wendy had not been dragged into this. Then Wendy coughed and wiped her bloodied lip and I looked at her. She had a black eye, and her eyes were red from crying and I looked at her hands as she slightly moved them, it looked as if the rope had burned her wrists and may even be bleeding.

"Brice help me untie her now." I said as I fell forward, out of my chair and grabbed at her hands. Brice leaned down and did the best that he could to help me, but I could tell he was in fact dizzy.

We broke Wendy's hands free and then I looked at her and placed my hand on her face. She laid her hand over mine and closed her eyes and then the door swung open and we all looked up to see a dark shadow of a man who moved slowly into the light of the candles and I gritted my teeth as I stared at Drake.

"You dick." I muttered.

Drake shook his head and grinned at me as he pulled out a gun and let the light play off of it. I stared at it and wondered how many he had killed and then he spoke.

"You are so pathetic, I swear Jude." he said, half mocking me.

I pushed myself towards my chair and Brice helped me up while Drake stared at the three of us. I leaned back and then stared Drake down with as much hatred as I could muster up in me.

"Jude . . . . Jude . . . . Jude." Drake sang out.

I shook my head and glanced at Wendy, who looked completely terrified.

"Trying to be superman I see." Drake added.

I laughed, not because I thought it was really funny . . . I guess it was more of a nervous laugh.

"Drake, listen. You got the money, let us go." I said.

Drake smiled and tapped the gun to his temple.

"You really expected me to do that didn't you?"

I reached my hand out to Wendy and she took it and stood up next to me.

"So what now? You keep us here?" she asked him.

Drake laughed again.

"Keep you here? Are you offering to go to work for me Wendy? I mean, I could use another whore, but you need some work."

"Shut up." I said.

Drake looked back at me and grinned.

"You just can't help yourself can you? Always having sex with trouble."

"Drake I swear to god, let us go."

Drake started to pace in the room then he turned the gun on Brice.

"For a price." he said.

Brice raised his eyebrows at him.

"You have your money, what else do you want?" he said.

"A life." he added.

I swallowed and felt Wendy tighten her grip on my hand.

"What? You want to kill me? Fine, do it and let them go." Brice said.

I looked at Brice completely shocked that he offered.

Drake nodded and looked at me. Then he squeezed the trigger and Brice made no sound as he hit the floor. He twitched for a moment and then started to relax. I screamed out and so did Wendy and we both reached him just as he started to try to talk. I leaned down and tried to hear him.

"I am sorry Valerie my love." he whispered and then he took a short breath and he was gone. I pressed my hand to his chest and the blood ran up over my fingers and Wendy started to sob. I slammed my fist against his chest and nothing, then I hit him again and by the 5th or 6th time Wendy caught my hand and shook her head at me. I reached up and closed his eyes and then my anger settled on Drake as I stared him down like the demon he was.

Drake tapped the gun on his pants and then waved it around in the air.

"Who first?" he asked us.

I shook my head and looked at Wendy and she bit her lip. I looked back at Drake.

"You said 'a life' . . . you got that, let us go." I said.

Drake stopped pacing and stared at the two of us and then looked at Brice.

"He doesn't count, he sucked." Drake said.

"Brice may have had his problems, but he did not deserve to die."

"Oh you think?" Drake screamed out and it echoed in the room.

"Listen I don't know what he did to you, or how much money he owed you, but he did not deserve this." I said.

Drake doubled over laughing.

"Jude! You are an idiot man! Brice was a bastard, his daughter was a whore and you are the dumb shit who just had to start banging her."

"What?"

Drake ran to us and grabbed Wendy's hand, he jerked her away from me as I yelled out and he wrapped his arm around her and held her to him, facing me. He placed the gun to her head and she sobbed.

"I have a little story for you, one I would like for you to hear before I send you to hell." he said.

"Drake calm down, please let Wendy go."

Drake shook her and she yelled out then he grinned at me.

"I know you know about Val and I."

"In the past dude." I said.

"No . . . no, never in the past man! You see I got that bitch pregnant Jude and her Daddy took my son away from me, so to make him understand just how cool that WAS NOT! I took the one thing he loved away from him."

"What are you saying?" I asked him.

"I killed that bitch Jude . . . I am the reason Val is dead."

I sat there and the room spinned. I felt like throwing up immediately and I bent over thinking that I would. Drake loosened his grip on Wendy, then he hit her and she fell to the ground as she cried out. I could not seem to straighten up at all as the pain in my stomach held me frozen. Drake walked towards me and I peeked up at him as he smiled.

Drake . . . the man who served me alcohol, the man who listened to me before and after Valerie. The man who killed Brice and my Val, my Val . . . .

Drake leaned down and that is when I did what I never thought I would do, I pulled out the gun and I placed it right under his chin and smiled at him.

"See you in hell." I said and I pulled the trigger and blew the back of head off. He flew away from me and hit the floor and Wendy screamed and covered her mouth.

"Oh God . . . . oh God . . . . Jude! What did you do?" she sobbed.

"Roll me to that window." I said, suddenly not feeling anything at all.

She stumbled as she stood up and I yelled at her.

"Now!"

She jumped and rolled me the window and I handed her the gun.

"Break it." I said.

She hesitated and I yelled it again as I rolled back to Drake, who looked a mess and I reached into his pocket. I smiled as I pulled out his keys. I looked back at Wendy and she stood there with the gun in her hand like a deer in headlights. I rolled up to her.

"Pick me up and toss me out the window."

"What?" she said in a daze.

"Pick me up now!" I yelled at her and then the knocking on the door came.

"Boss? You done or what? We got a game starting." the voice said.

I looked at Wendy and something kicked in on her, probably a survival instinct that we all have. She started to lift me and she groaned.

"Stop fucking around." I said.

She moaned as she lifted me up and I gripped the side of the window sill and cut my hands. I ignored it, in fact it felt like nothing to me.

The banging on the door came again and then a hard hit, and another. I pulled with everything that I had as Wendy pushed me and I fell over the top and onto the concrete, knocking the wind out of me. Wendy followed quickly as the door was busted in and she ducked just as the first shots rang out.

"Shit . . . left my chair!" I said and Wendy stood up half way, grabbed me as bullets flew by her and drug me to the car. She got me in first and a bullet clipped her arm and she screamed and dropped to the ground.

"Get in or die!" I yelled at her.

Somehow she felt the power in her to stand up and run to the drivers side. I tossed her the keys and she started the car as her hand shook.

The doors to the warehouse flew open and the shots started to hit the car as Drake's men ran towards us. Then she got the car started and I looked at her . . .

"Run . . . as fast and as hard as you can!"

She slammed her foot on the gas and I looked back at Brice and Drake's final resting place and tried to push Val's memory from me forever . . . .